HER LESSON IN LOVE

HEIDI LOWE

Copyright © 2016 Heidi Lowe

The right of Heidi Lowe to be identified as the author of this work has been asserted by her in accordance with the Copyright, Designs and Patents Act 1988.

All rights reserved.

First published in 2016 by Heidi Lowe Books.

ISBN: 1540614042
ISBN-13: 978–1540614049

ONE

I didn't bother knocking before I entered the room. My husband lay passed out on his bed, the sheets in a heap on the floor. I switched on the light and he stirred awake.

"Huh?" He squinted at me as his eyes adjusted to the light. "What's going on?"

"It's almost half five. We have to get going," I said impatiently.

"Where?"

I tutted. Of course he'd forgotten. Leave it up to Dominic to forget something as important as this.

"The parent-teacher conference. You promised Chester you would go, remember?"

"I did?" His voice was groggy, filled with sleep.

"Yeah, you did. But go ahead, miss this too. I'm sure our son's used to that by now."

Now it was his turn to tut. Well, at least my petulance had succeeded in waking him.

"You couldn't wait to get that in, could you? Always so damn negative. Close the door behind you. I'll be down in ten minutes."

I didn't stay around to argue. I wasn't in the mood, and Chester was downstairs. We'd thus far managed to shield him from our arguments – putting on a smile and a front whenever he was about, just so our seven-year-old son wouldn't realize his parents despised each other.

I went back to my bedroom to change my shirt, having noticed the stain on it. It must have happened when I was making the pasta sauce. Dominic and Chester were waiting for me in Dominic's car when I came downstairs. Chester was sitting in the back, staring miserably out of the window.

"What's up, champ?" I asked as I strapped myself in.

"What if the new teacher is mean, Mom?" he asked, turning to look at me with his huge green eyes. He'd gotten those from me. The shaggy dark-brown hair, too.

"I'm sure they wouldn't hire someone mean, honey. Don't worry."

"They did before."

Dominic laughed as he started the car. "No one could be as bad as old coffee-breath Mrs. Wickham."

I shot him a look but said nothing. The truth was my son had had really bad luck with teachers in that school. The school itself had a good reputation – one of the highest rated in the state of Virginia. But there must have been a curse on his class, because they couldn't hold onto a teacher, and when they did they were usually useless. As one of a dying number of schools that practiced looping, he had no chance of getting one of the other teachers the following year. The one he'd had last semester had left to teach in Europe.

The fifteen minute drive was relatively quiet; Chester did most of the talking. Dominic and I found it easier this way, saying nothing to each other, knowing that this was the only way to avoid fighting.

Once Dominic had parked, I took Chester's hand and walked ahead, leaving my husband to trail behind. I nodded a hello to a cluster of mothers I knew, who were standing at the entrance sharing a cigarette and gossip.

Davenport Elementary School buzzed with life as pupils of all grades had gathered for the parent-teacher conference, an event that took place here the week before the new school year began. There were kids and adults in every corner, it seemed. Dominic hated this sort of thing, always said he could be making money instead of wasting valuable time standing around like a sheep. Those day trader types never saw the value in doing anything but trading stocks. Well, that and, in Dominic's case, screwing college students half his age behind my back.

We walked along the corridor, saying hello to people we knew, exchanging brief words, until we reached Chester's classroom. Several parents were already inside with their children and the vice-principal.

"Danielle, hi." A friend, and the mother of one of Chester's classmates, embraced me as soon as I walked in. She gave me air kisses to both cheeks.

"Beth, look at you, you look great! Exotic," I said, giving her the once-over. "That vacation seems to have done you good." She just happened to be wearing the most revealing outfit I'd ever seen on her, with lots of flesh on display to show off her golden skin. I couldn't remember the last time I'd had a real vacation, or a tan that didn't come in a bottle.

"Thanks. I got back a couple of days ago."

Chester and Dominic had wandered off to do a lap of the room, examining all the projects the class had done over the past year.

"What's going on? I thought we were going to meet the new teacher tonight."

"That's what the principal said. She hasn't come in yet, I don't think. If she's late, great start to her new job."

"So it's another woman?"

"Just a guess," she said. "They're always women. By the way, we have to get together soon. I wore one of your necklaces when I was away. A lot of people were interested in your designs. I gave them a link to your website, I hope that's all right?"

Free publicity? Heck yeah it was all right! Sales had been slow lately, thanks to the recession, so this was good news. When you're trying to scrape together money to make mortgage payments, buying homemade jewelry is the last thing on your list of priorities.

It seemed like all heads turned at once when the door opened and a woman walked in. Now, this wasn't just any woman. No one among us had ever seen her before, and certainly weren't expecting her. It's hard to say what I noticed about her first: the long, flowing blonde locks that fell past her breasts; the super svelte figure that could have jumped straight out of a swimsuit magazine; or the immaculate white smile behind full cherry-red lips. I'm sure there were more than a few dropped jaws in the room, mine being one of them. Her entrance even managed to stop Beth mid-sentence.

It was as though no one quite knew what to do next. Had she gotten lost on her way to the catwalk? No, she seemed to be in the right place, judging by the comfortable and easy way she strutted across the room. She said a shy hello to everyone, giving a blinding smile. *She must be a parent*, I thought. *But where's her child?*

The vice-principal stepped forward. "Hi folks. I'd like to introduce you to Miss Petal. She'll be taking over this class when the new school year starts next week."

A bunch of nervous hellos followed. I imagined everyone was gawking at her still; but I couldn't tell, I was too busy doing the same myself.

I saw her cheeks light up a little, so everyone else must

have seen that too. I wondered if she was real or a figment of our collective imaginations. Either that or someone was playing an elaborate trick on us. Because if this was to be my son's new teacher, then holy hell! They didn't make teachers like that when I was a girl. They were all old, gray, with huge wire-rimmed glasses, and hideous knitted sweaters.

And her name: Miss Petal. Yeah, what a joke! She might as well have been called Miss Beautiful, Miss Stunning, Miss Perfect, any of which would have suited her to a T.

A couple of minutes later, once everyone had (mostly) picked their jaws up off the floor, she was making her rounds, shaking hands with all the parents, and getting to know some of her future students.

There's something very predatory about what happens to a group of women when a much younger, much prettier version steps into the room. We become like a pack of vultures, eyes turning to slits of jealousy, not even aware of how quickly we've changed. And I must admit, I'd been guilty of that type of thing in the past.

"Look at her. That laugh is so fake." This came from Miranda, another mother and friend of mine, who'd come to stand with me and Beth. It did not surprise me one iota to hear something like that from her. The woman couldn't go more than five minutes without being bitchy.

"I know, right! Nobody's really that nice. Oh God, just look how the men are fawning over her. It's disgusting!" Beth added. We'd huddled into a corner to stare and pass judgment on a woman we hadn't even met yet. Normally I would have joined in, offered my own malicious observations, but something came over me that evening.

"Teacher my eye! What's she going to teach my daughter, how to do make up and look good for guys?" Miranda went on. "And you'd better watch your husband, Dani. He looks like he's getting a little too familiar there."

I *was* looking at him, and it was exactly as she said. Nothing I hadn't seen before. If they wanted to talk about fake smiles, Dominic was the master of them. He was probably trying to impress her enough to add her to his ever-expanding list of extramarital affairs. My husband – the Lothario. He wasn't even trying to flirt subtly.

"Yeah, I'm a day trader. Work from home, you know, that sort of thing. Set my own hours, do what I want. It does get a little lonely though, not having co-workers, but what can you do?" I heard part of the exchange – the slimy, self-conceited rambling of a married man who'd seemingly forgotten that, not only was he married, but his wife and son were in the room!

I looked away, embarrassed. I'd seen him do it so many times, but with our friends around it really got to me. Not jealousy, not really. Just embarrassment that I couldn't keep my husband in check.

"Oh, and there goes Fred," Beth said. "Looks like your husband's fallen under the same spell, Miranda."

Miranda scowled. "They don't know how pathetic they all look. Like they actually stand a chance. I know Fred certainly doesn't, unless she's into boring, prematurely balding, slightly overweight insurance brokers!"

We all laughed, although I didn't have much to laugh about. It was no secret that I'd hit the jackpot when I married Dominic. Good-looking, great hair, successful, and from a good family. A real catch, the other moms said. And although it was never expressed, I got the feeling they were surprised by my ability to bag him and hold on to him. They didn't know that, after six years of marriage, I had never truly succeeded. He'd been a cheat from day one and still was. But I'd managed to keep the affairs a secret from everyone.

"Ugh, she's coming over here. And there I was thinking she was only interested in speaking to the men in the room."

Before I knew it Beth and Miranda had hightailed it to their husbands just as Miss Petal made a beeline for me.

"Hi." She offered me her hand, and I gave it a light shake. Her skin was so soft. "Miss Petal. And you are?"

"I, uh..." I stumbled, unable to locate the words to speak. My gaze was lost in the bluest eyes I'd ever seen; a unique, striking shade, like sapphire and gray combined. Her lashes were long. When I finally found my voice again, it came out tiny. "Danielle. Danielle Thomas."

"Ah, so you're Chester's mom? I just met him. He seems great. I'm looking forward to teaching him."

She'd probably used that line half a dozen times already, and hadn't meant one word of it. But she made it sound genuine. I found myself truly mystified, waiting for her to speak again. She had the softest voice and a melodic accent – southern in some places, but a hint of something else also.

"Your accent, where's it from?" I said as casually as I could manage. It took me a while to realize that my eyes kept drifting to her lips – bee-stung, glistening, her lipstick perfectly applied. Was there anything at all that wasn't perfect about this woman? My inferiority complex started kicking in big style.

She smiled even wider, keeping eye contact the whole time. "Georgia mostly, but I've lived all over. Army kid. You know how it is."

"Yeah, I have heard. But you plan on sticking around for awhile at least?" Only once the question had come out did I realize it was more than a little nosy. She was well within her rights to ignore it, tell me to mind my own business, and flit off to converse with some other parents. So I added quickly, "You know, because this class hasn't been able to hold onto a teacher. It would be nice if, just once, there was some stability."

I wanted to kick myself. I sounded like one of those obnoxious mothers who interfered way too much. I didn't want her to think I would constantly be on her back.

She let out a small laugh, seemingly unfazed by my words. "I quite like it here in Davenport. I'm not planning on going anywhere, so you can rest easy." She laughed again.

I just watched her, unable to take my eyes off her. What a fascinating specimen. Elegant, attractive, smelled like candy. She couldn't have come out any better had she been designed.

"Well, it was nice meeting you, Mrs. Thomas. Maybe we'll talk again later. I can't wait to get to know you when I start." She excused herself, moved on to another set of parents. And as I followed her with my gaze, I couldn't help thinking the same: I was anxious for her to start next week. Only, I had no idea why.

"So, Miss Petal seems really nice," Dominic said. We were on our way home that evening. It was the second time he'd said it and, knowing him, the hundredth time he'd thought it. His definition of nice, sadly, included a little more than just personality. He would have noticed her impressive bosom, or the pert, round butt you could bounce a quarter off! If I had, he certainly had too.

"I like her," Chester chimed in. "She smells nice, too."

I rolled my eyes as I looked out the window. Men. Even my son had been sucked in by her charms. But, well, she *did* smell nice.

"Finally our son will have a decent teacher."

I turned a scathing look at Dominic. "How do you know that? You just met the woman."

"I have a good feeling about this one."

I rolled my eyes again. *And did that feeling happen to start somewhere in your groin, perhaps?* I wondered. He was so transparent it was almost funny. Why didn't he just say he wanted to get into her pants, and stop with the ambiguous comments? I would have thought a little more of him.

TWO

"Mom, we're gonna be late. Come on!" Chester called from the bottom of the stairs.

"Honey, it won't make me go any faster if you keep saying that," I called back, flinging open my drawers, trying to locate a pair of stockings, which was surprisingly difficult. I rarely wore them, but it was chilly out. I also hadn't shaved my legs in a week (one of the perks of being separated) and didn't have time to do so now. My alarm had failed to wake me (because I'd failed to set it!) and, as a result, Chester, too, had overslept. We were running late for the first day of the new school year.

"I'm gonna get detention," he complained.

"I'll explain to Miss Petal that it was my fault. I'm sure she'll make an exception this once."

I managed to find a pair, and slipped them on as quickly as possible. My heart raced at a speed it only ever hit when I was on the treadmill. Had my search for a pair of stockings really taken it out of me, or was something else causing the pounding in my chest?

I didn't have to think about it too long. Today was the day, Miss Petal's first day. And I was shaking like a leaf as though it was *my* first day of school.

For the past week I'd been eagerly awaiting this moment, when she would become a permanent fixture at my son's school, and thus a permanent fixture in our lives. My life. I couldn't figure out where this intrigue was coming from. It also explained the alarm mishap. I'd been unable to sleep properly the night before, getting only a couple of hours in, and unfortunately forgot to switch on the alarm.

I'd never been this excited, or this nervous, to go to school. I tried to convince myself that my new-found enthusiasm for doing the school run had everything to do with regaining my freedom during the day, and nothing to do with the newest member of Davenport Elementary School's faculty.

I knew when I was lying to myself, and now was one of those times. My heart beat just a little faster as I remembered, and not for the first time, those sapphire-blue eyes, so inviting and hypnotizing.

"Mom!" Chester yelled.

"Jesus, Chester, all right. I'm going as fast as I can. You don't want Mommy to get a ladder in her stocking, do you?" *Mommy also doesn't want Mommy to get a ladder*, I thought. What sort of impression would that give Miss Petal?

He didn't respond with words, just a really loud growl. I suspected he didn't much care how I turned up to school, just that we got there some time this week.

I heard Dominic's bedroom door open. He'd been getting up later and later the past few months, staying out long into the early hours the night before, most likely with some bimbo.

"What's going on?" he said, his voice groggy.

"It's Monday morning, first day of the new semester. What do you think?" I grumbled. Almost ready. And if I hadn't been, the waking of my husband would have hurried me along. Talking to him was an exercise in self-torture sometimes.

"That's today? Don't they usually go back on a Tuesday?"

"Not this semester."

He was at my door in nothing but his boxers, rubbing sleep from his eyes. Once upon a time it would have pained me to walk away from that body – still impressively toned, though thicker in the stomach area now, due to over-consumption of beer and fast food. Now I had no such trouble. He didn't even feel like mine to enjoy anymore; and I often wondered how many others were currently doing so.

"You should have woken me, Danielle. I said I was happy to take him."

"I've been doing it almost every day since he started school. No use stopping now." Finished. I grabbed my jacket, slipped it on.

"Still, I said I would. You're just being petty when you thwart my attempts to take a more active role in our son's life. You complain that I don't, and when I want to, this is what I get."

I laughed humorlessly. "Maybe I wouldn't have such a problem with this new and sudden dedication to your son's education if I didn't know about your ulterior motive." I lowered my voice so Chester wouldn't hear.

"What ulterior motive? You need help, you know that? You get these insane ideas into your head and just run along with them."

"Okay, so I'm wrong in thinking that the only reason you're suddenly interested in being a father is because of our son's hot new teacher?"

"See, out of your mind! You think I want every piece of ass that crosses my path. That's on you, not me." I always knew when I'd caught him in a lie – his voice went up in pitch.

"Don't give me that crap. You've been making little comments about her all week."

"Just taking an interest in our son's education."

"Whatever, Dominic. Step aside, I'm already late." I practically had to shove him aside as I left the room, because he seemed unwilling to let me pass without a struggle.

"You wouldn't be so insecure if you were putting out yourself. Just saying."

What an asshole! I should have left it alone, but he riled me up so much that I had to have the final word.

"Put out? To you? No thanks. I'd rather not play the STI lottery again!"

My impatient son was all but tapping his foot at the bottom of the stairs. "I'm definitely going to get detention now."

"I'll square it with Miss Petal," I promised, and my stomach did a leap at the thought.

As we approached the classroom, I could already hear her voice addressing the class. Thud, thud went my heart.

"What if she doesn't let me in?" Chester said. "Some of the other teachers do that when their pupils are late."

I didn't answer him. Even though I had no idea what type of person Miss Petal was beneath that smile and those warm, beckoning eyes, I wanted to believe that she was kindhearted. Someone with the face of an angel couldn't possibly be a tyrant who punished kids for their parents' lateness, surely?

I peered through the glass screen on the door, saw her at the front of the room. I watched for a few seconds before tapping lightly. She stopped talking, and the whole class turned to the door.

"Come in," she called in the sweetest voice. We entered tentatively. "Good morning." She smiled at us, at me. God, that smile. How many hearts had she melted with it? How many more had she yet to melt? I felt my own dissolve as I stared at her.

"Hi. I'm so sorry we're late. It's my fault. My alarm didn't go off. I'm sorry," I said, flustered.

"Hmm, I thought there was someone missing this morning."

"This won't happen again, I promise." I nudged my son into the room.

"I'll take your word for it. We like punctuality in this class, don't we, guys?"

As one, the class said yes.

"I give out detentions to parents too, Mrs. Thomas." The class laughed, and she winked at me.

It was all too overwhelming. Not only had she remembered my name, she'd made a joke and...*winked* at me! Who was this woman and why did I suddenly feel light-headed when I looked at her?

"Uh, right. Like I said, it won't happen again. I'll be on my way now."

"Bye." She did a little wave, and I got a glimpse of my son's face in the crowd: red with embarrassment. I was obviously cramping his style.

I left hurriedly, though leaving was the last thing I wanted to do. Oh to have been seven years old again, to be in the second grade with a teacher like that. But where were these thoughts coming from? Was it just admiration for an attractive woman doing an amazing job? Yes, it had to be that.

I hung outside the room, catching my breath, getting my heartbeat down to a normal speed.

"Okay, so where were we? My name begins with a P – Petal. P is also for paper. Now we'll go around the room saying our name, saying the first letter of it, and then choosing something that also begins with that letter. Does everyone understand?"

I could play that game. D for desire – the desire to trade places with your seven-year-old son. Or D for deranged – what you are for *wanting* to trade places with your seven-year-old-son!

I stood outside that room peering inside, listening as the students answered enthusiastically, jokes and laughter ensuing. For a couple of minutes this went on, and I forgot all about the chores I had to do, about the jewelry orders I needed to fulfill. Nothing else seemed more important than being here, watching her work.

I thought I was well hidden, that because of the way the glass was made it would be difficult for anyone to see out at me. But when she started towards the door, I turned and tried to sneak away.

"Mrs. Thomas, you're still here?" Too late. She'd opened the door and caught me.

I looked at her guiltily. "Hi, uh...I...uh..."

"Were you spying on me?" she asked, eyes and voice full of amusement.

I felt my cheeks burn. "No, of course not, I–"

She laughed. "I'm kidding." She touched my arm lightly as a way to relax me. It did exactly the opposite. "I get it, you're a concerned mother who wants to see how well I perform. I would be curious too. Please, come in. There's a seat at the back if you want to watch for a little while."

My legs were carrying me without my permission. I avoided eye contact with Chester, who I imagined wanted to kill me by then.

I stayed for fifteen minutes, trying to be as inconspicuous as possible. I watched and listened with fascination. Observed how at ease she was at the front of the room, and how mesmerized they all were. She was the complete package: funny, confident, learned and beautiful.

They loved her, and my God, it was easy to see why.

THREE

"And Miss Petal says before we were monkeys we lived in the sea and had gills and everything."

"And Miss Petal says that in a hundred thousand years humans will have evolved into something else, and we will look different than we do now."

"And Miss Petal says there are many different species living on the other planets."

It had been going on like that for two weeks, ever since her arrival. Breakfasts and dinners progressed the same, with Chester rambling about everything he'd learned in class, never forgetting to drop his teacher's now famous name in, reminding me of her existence.

The thing was, I didn't need a reminder. I saw her every day when I dropped him off and picked him up. I saw the smile. The golden tresses of soft blonde hair. The enviously svelte body. The difference now, as opposed to with past teachers, was that I eagerly anticipated these brief moments in her presence. The sneaky little glances I took when she wasn't looking. Or the little smiles we exchanged when she caught me looking. I'd blushed so much around her, she must have thought that was my permanent color!

"Wow, someone really likes Miss Petal, huh?" I said to my

son that morning, after yet another of his monologues about his great and wonderful new teacher.

"She's awesome. And she has an amazing voice when she sings."

Of course she can sing too, I thought, doing an internal eye roll. What else could she do, heal the sick? Turn water into wine? He'd told me and Dominic last week, when we helped him on his hobbies essay, that she used to be a gymnast. A pro, he'd said, competing in competitions until her late teens.

"Really?" I'd watched Dominic's eyebrows rise with intrigue. "A gymnast? And does she still practice? She must be pretty flexible..."

I didn't need him to spell out what was on his dirty mind. The guy was like an open book – the sort that should have been banned or burned!

"She used to be in the choir at school. She says we're going to start a class rock band. So cool," Chester went on. I'd taught him not to speak with his mouth full, but when it came to Miss Petal, his favorite subject, he couldn't contain himself. Cereal sprayed everywhere as he chatted animatedly.

"I can't wait to eat some of Miss Petal's cake today at the bake sale. It's chocolate."

"I thought you didn't like chocolate cake, honey."

"But Miss Petal's one will be nice. I just know it."

I held back a laugh. Like father, like son.

"Should we take the cookies with us now, or should I bring them this afternoon when we set up the stall?"

He shrugged and went on talking about his teacher. If I were any other mother, Beth or Miranda especially, I would have banned mention of her name under my roof by now. But for some reason I enjoyed learning about Miss Petal's life, without her knowing. It felt a little sneaky, even though I wasn't sending Chester to her to extract the information. He couldn't answer the more pertinent questions, however, like: did she move here alone? How old was she? Was there a man in her life? None of that was my business, nor could I figure out why it even mattered to me.

I would have to do some digging of my own. And the bake sale was the perfect opportunity for that.

Parents and students circled and hovered around the various stalls, on which sat treats of all kinds – from homemade toffee to fancy cupcakes. I counted twenty-five tables, including mine and Chester's. Everyone had gone to a lot of trouble, like they did every year. It was sort of a big deal for the school, something mothers planned weeks in advance, practicing new recipes, trying to perfect them in time for the bake sale. All proceeds went to charity, so everyone was happy.

I'd opted for my snowflake cookies, which had always been a hit.

"Mmm, you have to give me this recipe," Beth said, munching on her third one. She didn't mind dropping several dollars on these, and insisted I just sell the whole batch to her.

I laughed. "You ask me that every time I make these. It's a trade secret. If I told you I'd have to kill you."

She pouted. "What a horrible person you are! I can't believe we're friends."

"Are we friends?" I joked. "I thought our kids were friends. You and I just tolerate each other."

After insisting that I was the worst person she'd ever met, then telling me she'd be back to gossip in ten minutes, she left me to go hunt down some more treats. The way she ate, she should have been the size of a castle!

I saw Chester in the crowd with a couple of his friends, Beth's son Jack, and Miranda's daughter Emma. Typical. It was his bake sale, yet I'd been left to do the labor. Come to think of it, he hadn't helped much in the baking either.

I was lost in thought, wondering whether I'd been unwittingly raising my son to be just like his father, when I looked up and saw Miss Petal approaching my table. Her strap dress was a light yellow and flowed when she walked, just like her hair.

"Hi." She beamed at me, white teeth gleaming.

"Hello." There was a frog in my throat. When I cleared it I said it again.

She looked down at the sign on the table. "Snowflake cookies. Yummy." I watched her tongue pass across her bottom lip, and I couldn't tear my eyes away. "I just heard some of the other parents talking about them." She reached into her purse, a little one she wore across her shoulder. She took out two dollar bills. "One, please."

I took the money from her, picked up a napkin and handed her a cookie. "If they're as delicious as everyone says they are, I might take the whole lot."

"Actually, there's a three per customer rule."

"Really? Wow, they must be something special."

My intention hadn't been to watch her eat, but that was precisely what I did. I watched her take her first bite, with those succulent red lips. It seemed to happen in slow motion. I wanted her to like it; love it. Her approval was suddenly extremely important to me.

"Oh my God, this is like a bite of Heaven!"

Approved.

I laughed. "I'm glad you like it."

"Like it? I love it." She gobbled and gobbled the rest down, moaning with delight after every mouthful. The whole thing sounded a little x-rated. Too sexy for this setting. Or was that just my lecherous mind making me think that?

"Now I understand why there's a three per customer rule. I

think I'll take two more, take them home with me."

My curiosity was piqued. Who was she taking them home for, herself or the male model I suspected she was dating? In my head she lived in this fancy, expensive apartment in the upmarket part of town, drove an expensive car, and had a rich, hunky boyfriend to fit her perfectly beautiful life. That image didn't exactly fit with the woman standing before me now, however; munching away at one of my cookies, she seemed completely unconcerned by how she looked, or what anyone thought of her.

I wrapped a couple more up and took her money. I felt like giving them all to her for free! She probably had that effect on many people.

"Hey, I adore your necklace. Where did you get it?" she said.

"I made it. That's what I do. Make jewelry no one wants, then spend my life trying to convince them they can't live without it."

She chuckled. "So you make jewelry *and* you can bake? And the rest of us mere mortals have to settle for being ordinary."

Was she teasing me? There were many things this woman was, but ordinary wasn't one of them.

I snorted, then spoke before I could stop myself. "Says the lady who sings, used to be a gymnast, and once beat Serena Williams in a friendly game of tennis."

Oh, dear God! What the hell was I thinking coming out with that stuff? Well, that was just it, I *wasn't* thinking. Why had Chester shared that information with me? And, more importantly, why had I retained it?

She looked at me with narrowed eyes, a little smirk at the corner of her mouth. "Well, that's just not fair. You know all about me, but I know nothing about you, Mrs. Thomas."

She put a hand on her hip, and she looked and sounded

like a true southern belle, her accent becoming more pronounced, more singsong in her amusement.

"I'm sorry. Chester goes on and on about you. It's Miss Petal this, Miss Petal that." There was no way she missed my blush.

She chuckled. "I know what children are like, don't worry about it. Chester's a great kid."

"Do you have kids?" I silently praised myself on the natural transition into the topic of her marital status.

"Oh no." She shook her head quickly, as though the idea was absurd. "Motherhood's a long way off for me."

"And your boyfriend, he feels the same...?"

"Well, if I had one he might." Her smile was daring, as though she knew the casual tone I'd been trying for was forced.

So she was single. The world truly didn't make sense. What was the saying? *If a beautiful woman is single, she must be crazy.* Misogynistic drivel, but it did get me thinking. Maybe she was between relationships. Or perhaps had come out of a bitter divorce just recently. Who was I to question why she was single? I knew better than most what trouble men were. If anything, she was the sane one.

I wanted to grill her further, but one of the dads came over to the table. I knew immediately that he had no intention of buying anything, and that Miss Petal was his target. This wasn't an isolated incident. In fact it was a regular occurrence, something I'd witnessed numerous times. The men would hover around her like bees to nectar, like moths to light bulbs. Flirted outrageously, offering to do things for her, always one overzealous compliment away from being creepy.

"If you come down to the garage, we can do you a deal, no problem."

"My friend owns a restaurant in town. Nice place. Just let me know when you wanna go down there and you can eat there free of charge. It might only work if I'm with you, though..."

Yeah, they really were that slimy. Married men flirting with their kids' teacher. How pathetic. I wondered what Dominic would offer her? He'd probably offer to add her to his hedge fund or something, promising to make her filthy, stinking rich.

"See ya, Mrs. Thomas," Miss Petal said, and walked off with the man. I shook my head, and didn't realize I'd folded my arms until Chester came to the table and asked me why I was sulking.

I really didn't want to consider the answer to that.

FOUR

"I've never seen you in that shirt before."

Dominic's voice startled me. I didn't know I'd left my door open. How long had he been standing there watching me change?

It was a Saturday afternoon and I was headed into town to the local bookstore. One of my favorite authors was doing a book-signing for her latest release. I'd been eagerly awaiting this event the past three months, and when I got excited like this about something it usually meant at least five outfit changes to get the right look for the day.

"It's new," I said, dismissively. What the hell was he doing in my room anyway? He still thought he had a right to let himself in whenever he wanted.

"Can I see it from the front?"

"Why?"

"Because."

Oh, I knew what this was. High libido, none of his floozies around to satisfy his appetite, so he had to look to his wife as a last resort. His wife, who'd had to endure his nasty comments about her very slight weight gain and anything else he could use to make her feel worthless. I was by no means fat, and the few pounds I'd gained had been through stress eating, thanks to his cheating.

"I don't have time to entertain you, Dominic. I'm sure you can find someone else to do that for you."

"We're still married, you know. Sometimes I think you forget that." I heard the agitation in his voice.

"*Me?*" Now I had to look at him, unable to believe the audacity. "Talk about pot calling the kettle black."

"Oh enough about the women. Let go of the past. God, you sound like a broken record. And you wonder why I felt the need to look elsewhere."

Had he come in here to screw me or screw with me? Because these comments, they were causing more shock than anger in me. Maybe he was taking his opportunity to fight now that Chester was at a friend's for the day.

But I didn't have the time or energy to deal with his nonsense. I had a book-signing to get to.

"And with an attitude like that, you wonder why I'm never letting you near me again."

"Never's a long time, Dani. And you're not getting any younger."

All I could do was shake my head as I stepped past him and left the room. Obnoxious jerk. Once upon a time I'd mistaken that for mere confidence, and I'd found it sexy. Now I couldn't stand to be in the same house as him let alone the same room.

My intention had been to get to the store early, to be close to the beginning of the line. Once I'd parked my car and walked in, I took a look at the line and my heart sank. It was about thirty people strong. I had no idea the author was so popular. And no doubt there were still more to come.

I picked up a copy of the book and joined the end of the line. At least I could read while I waited.

Of the thirty or so people, I spotted only one man, and he looked to be accompanied by a woman – his girlfriend probably, who'd dragged him along. No surprise considering the material this author wrote about. Her latest novel, the reviews said, was as anti-men as they came, and not for the faint of heart. While I didn't hate men, my dislike for my husband put me in the right frame of mind to enjoy a book like that. I couldn't wait to read it. And to finally meet the woman behind the stories.

I peered up the line, which hadn't begun to move yet as the author hadn't arrived. About five places from the front, I spotted something that made my stomach lurch. The blonde hair of the woman with her back to me. I felt stupid seconds later. There were hundreds of millions of people with blonde hair in the world. Not everyone was Miss Petal.

I almost laughed out loud. Silly. I'd been seeing her everywhere, or should I say *imagining* her everywhere. Behind the counter at one of our local burger joints, in the bank, driving a taxi... It was stupid, obsessive.

And then the woman in front turned around. My heart leaped, felt like it would tear through my chest. This time, it was the real thing.

When her eyes landed on me, she beamed, waved energetically, then ushered me over. A chance to skip the line? Hell yeah I would take it.

The looks we received when I joined her weren't very nice, but I didn't care.

"I never thought I would see someone I know here. She's not a very well known writer in this town," I said. I still couldn't believe one of my crazy sightings had actually been true, and that I was now standing beside the real Miss Petal. It was like meeting royalty.

"Oh, I love her. Been a fan of her work since I was a

teenager. Got me through some tough times."

I wanted to hear all about those tough times, but just then the famous woman made her entrance, sat behind her table and the signing commenced.

There'd been a whole talk scheduled, but it was canceled the night before due to the author's other commitments. So once Miss Petal and I had gotten our books signed, and exchanged a few words with the woman, we made our way to the door.

She laughed. "Well, that was a bit anticlimactic."

"Yeah," I answered nervously. Around her I forgot how to converse. She must have thought I was the dullest person in town.

"You've probably got stuff to do, but I'll ask anyway. Do you wanna go for a coffee? There's a place just across the street."

"Yes!"

I don't think the words had completely left her mouth before I jumped in. It was so cringeworthy.

But as always she smiled brightly at me, so serene and perfect. Like a work of art you couldn't bear to tear your eyes away from. It should have been a crime to look as good as she did.

"Great." We set off across the street. "I don't really know anyone in town. I guess that's what happens when you move to a new state on your own."

The shop was a cozy little place with plush, comfy armchairs and a log fire. We got our coffees and found a couple of empty seats by the window. Even before she sat down, the stares from the men passing the shop began. She ignored them all. The young, the old, the hotties, the average. All of them. I saw them but she didn't.

Her eyes were on me, gleaming with intrigue. Then she

thrust her hand out at me. "I think now might be a good time to do this. I'm Ava."

I shook it. "Danielle."

Ava Petal. I couldn't think of a nicer sounding name. Or maybe it was only nice because it belonged to her. I really couldn't say.

"So, another L.V. Whiteside fan. There aren't many of us out there," I said after I'd taken a long drag on my coffee. I didn't even want it, but drank it because I was nervous.

"I don't know. The line was pretty big. I was expecting a much smaller turnout. She writes such controversial stuff."

My eyes automatically drifted to her lips as she sipped her drink, and they didn't avert until she looked up and caught me staring. I was simply terrible at this stealthy watching thing. But she only smiled. It must have happened to her all the time. The gawking, the objectifying. I wanted to be different, be the one that was cool around such beauty, but I was hopeless. I could see the two male baristas staring over in our direction. Definitely because of her, not me. In all my thirty-seven years no one had been impressed enough to stare like that at me.

"You mentioned that reading her books got you through some tough times," I said. One coffee wouldn't last very long, and I wanted to learn as much about her as possible. I had to act quickly.

"Oh, just my angsty teen years. I discovered her books at the right time, when I was discovering myself."

"Really? How so?"

She let out a nervous little laugh. "Well, I learned to accept the world and how I fit in it. When you're a teenager, it can get a little confusing, even dark. She was a light at the end of the tunnel."

How cryptic. It was obvious that she wanted to keep things

vague. Only problem was, her vagueness made me even more curious. I hoped one day we wouldn't be strangers anymore, that we would become such good friends that she wouldn't think twice about confiding in me. I didn't normally meet people I wanted to befriend; but there was something special about Miss Petal – about Ava – that made me want to keep her in my life.

"Well, I'm glad you found her. Do you read a lot?"

"All the time," she said enthusiastically. "I think it's a dying hobby. Most people my age would prefer to surf the internet or whatever twenty-eight year olds do these days." She chuckled. "I sound like a seventy-year-old grandmother, don't I?"

"Not at all. I love reading, too. If you were stranded on a desert island and you only had one book, what would it be?"

I'd asked that question a dozen times, and every person bar one replied that they wouldn't want to be stuck on an island with any book. I knew she wouldn't answer that way, but nothing could have prepared me for her reply.

"It would have to be Fannie Flagg's *Fried Green Tomatoes at the Whistlestop Cafe*."

I just gawped at her as if she were from outer space.

"What? I know, it's not a classic, not War and Peace or the Bible, but it has everything: murder, love, you name it."

"I, I know that... It's been my answer ever since I discovered and read the book as a teenager." I probably sounded spooked out. Of all the books ever written, we'd chosen the same one. Were we separated at birth?

"Well, isn't that something! Great minds. But I guess you and I probably wouldn't work well stranded on a desert island with that book. We would be fighting over who gets to read it."

We laughed.

"Or one of us would have to read it to the other. Problem

solved," she added.

She would be the one, since her voice was so melodic and gentle. I started imagining us on that island, around a fire, huddled close together, keeping warm. The image was beautiful for only a few seconds, until I realized that a grown woman fantasizing about that was weird.

We spent the next twenty minutes talking books, a subject most around us would have found boring, yet we spoke excitedly. I hadn't had this much fun in a long time.

Then she offered to buy me another coffee, and I found I couldn't say no. I had things to do at home, but this was more important. This was my duty as a mother, wasn't it? Convincing myself of that, that this was about Chester, allowed me to spend the afternoon in that cafe and not consider for even a minute the implications of my desire to be there with her.

"I think you have an admirer," I said. We'd been there for almost two hours and were on our third coffees. "Guy in the yellow coat. He's been looking over here since he came in."

She twisted around to see, and gave a look so brief I was certain she hadn't seen him. He smiled, but she was already turning back to me. "Not my type."

"Is it the jacket?"

"And everything else," she said quietly, sipping her drink.

"Sorry, I'm playing matchmaker again. I do this all the time."

"It's fine. I don't know what it is, people always want to set me up with guys they know."

Because you're gorgeous, and any guy who sees you will be eternally grateful for the match, I thought.

"It happens a lot?"

"More times than I'd like to admit. I mean, eventually they get the message, when they've known me long enough."

I got the feeling she was trying to say something, but I

couldn't figure out what it was.

"Trust your own judgment, that's a good motto. Well, unless you're me..."

She stared at me, her expression unreadable. "What do you mean?"

What *did* I mean? That I'd been foolish eight years ago with Dominic, thinking I would be the one to tame his bad boy ways? Or that even back then I'd known it wouldn't last, but had gone against my own wisdom and stuck it out this long anyway, just because I didn't want to hear I-told-you-so from my family?

"Marriage is hard, don't ever let anyone tell you otherwise." I laughed to try to recapture the carefree mood, but as often happened when the subject of my marriage cropped up, I became slightly wistful.

She looked down at her cup for awhile, and I could tell she wanted to say something, that she was holding back.

"But you've met my husband. You already know that. They're not all as bad as he is." Another laugh, even though I meant every word.

"I've spoken to him a couple of times, yes," she said. "He was at Chester's soccer game the other week."

Why wasn't she looking at me anymore? Immediately my mind jumped to the only obvious explanation for it, for her odd behavior now that we were on the subject of my marriage: she'd slept with my husband. And was this some sick game of hers to find out how strong we were, if he would ever leave me for her? I'd read enough books, and seen enough films to know how this stuff worked. Was the coffee her way of apologizing?

"Did you speak long?" I asked casually.

"Not really. A few minutes here and there. He seems nice."

"Oh, he is...with women. He's a bit of a playboy. Turns on

the charm with just about every pretty face he sees." If she thought she was special, that there hadn't already been many others before her, or that there wouldn't be any after her, she was in for a surprise.

Now she looked at me. "Why would he do a thing like that when he has such an amazing wife?"

She must have seen the shock in my eyes then, because she smiled. Okay, I was not expecting her to say *that*. If she had slept with my husband, this was a strange way of acting. And I knew I couldn't outright ask her.

"Flattering. But he doesn't think the way you do. Eight years together and six years of marriage makes you appreciate your partner less, I suppose."

She shook her head. "That's not how it works. If it's the right person, appreciation and true love last forever." She peered down at her cup again, then added, "At least that's what I've chosen to believe. And if your husband doesn't appreciate you then he's crazy. And undeserving..."

Whatever this woman was, I realized then that she wasn't sleeping with Dominic, and never would. I wanted to hug her for being immune to his charms. And for her compliments. She didn't know just how much her comments meant to me.

The silence must have become too awkward for her, because she peered up at the clock on the wall. "Would you look at the time. I totally lost track. I'm going to a book club meeting. It starts soon." She drained her cup and got to her feet.

"Oh, right. Of course. I've got a bunch of stuff to do at home before I collect Chester."

We put on our jackets.

"I had a great time," she said. "Thank you for indulging me in book-talk, my favorite topic. I'm still so new to town and I still don't know anyone, so it's nice to actually have someone here to talk to."

"You? I would have thought you wouldn't have any problems making friends." If *she* had difficulty, then what hope did the rest of us have?

"It's not easy for me. I'm shy, a bit of an introvert. With adults, but not with kids."

"You don't come off as shy to me." We walked to the door together.

She looked at me. "Well, not so much with you. You're a little different, Danielle. You make me feel at ease. We probably knew each other in another life." She laughed.

I just smiled. So she felt it too? That feeling of familiarity. That feeling didn't come around often, once or twice in a lifetime maybe. Some called it kindred spirits, but that was mostly in connection with lovers.

When we said our goodbyes, I didn't go straight home. I wandered the streets like a nomad, replaying the afternoon – from the meeting in the bookstore, and the way my heart leaped with excitement when she ushered me over, to our farewell hug. She'd instigated it. And I suspect, if she hadn't ended it herself, I would have kept my arms around her forever. She smelled delicious, felt wonderful.

Kindred spirits, huh? Well, it certainly felt that way.

FIVE

"**W**hy are you grinning like that? You went to a stupid book-signing," was the first thing Dominic said when I walked in an hour later. I hadn't realized I was smiling, but seeing his face and hearing his voice made sure all traces of the smile promptly vanished.

"It wasn't stupid. But then I wouldn't expect you to appreciate something like that."

After all the coffee I'd consumed, I was bursting to use the bathroom, and hurried away. I thought he would have disappeared by the time I came out, but he was lingering outside. Did he seriously still think I was going to sleep with him?

And then I had a genius idea to screw with him.

"I actually bumped into Chester's teacher there, so presumably she doesn't find book-signings stupid."

"Miss Petal?" He looked skeptical.

"Ah-huh. Ava. We had coffee." And dropping her first name in there like that felt terrific. I bet he wasn't on first name terms with her, and likely never would be, if her words were anything to go by.

"Why would she have coffee with you? What on earth did you both talk about?"

What he really wanted to know was if she'd mentioned

him. Because he, naturally, assumed that her only reason for wanting to spend time with me was because she was interested in him. A mistaken belief I'd once held. Not anymore, however.

"We have a lot in common," I said, smugness dripping from my every word.

"I find that hard to believe."

"Why? You don't know anything about her." I felt confident saying this, knowing it was the truth.

"What makes you think that? How do you know Miss Petal and I aren't very familiar?"

This was how much my husband respected me. He wanted me to think he'd cheated with Ava, all because of his male ego. It used to hurt before, when he first did it, when I cared. But now, I only looked at him pitifully and shook my head.

"She has more self-respect than your usual type. And from the way she spoke, it doesn't sound as if she agrees with infidelity." I grinned at him, loving the look on his face now. "So I'm afraid you're going to have to sniff around someone else's teacher, honey." I strutted away, leaving him glaring after me. I didn't think he would give up there, though. If he wanted something, or someone, he would just work harder to get it.

If she had been any other woman, I wouldn't have cared so much. But this one, Miss Petal, I prayed she didn't give in. I already valued our brand new friendship too much to want my husband corrupting it.

I wished I could have given the same talk to all the other married fathers.

"Maybe we should all dye our hair blonde, and get breast implants to make them perky and fresh. And put on an affected, over the top southern accent. Then our husbands might pay as much attention to us as they do to Miss Flower or whatever her name is over there."

Beth and I had just walked through the school gates, Chester and Jack having run off ahead of us. It was a bright, sunny morning and we'd decided to walk to school with the kids, leaving our gas-guzzling cars at home. Chester and I had met them en route.

In the playground, Miss Petal was in conversation with two fathers, one I was sure didn't have a child in her class! It had been like this for weeks; every day men who had rarely made the effort to bring their children to school would strike up a conversation with her. Over nothing, mostly. And every day I witnessed it, it turned my stomach.

"Don't be so mean," I said. Then turned to her in horror. "You don't really think she's had work done on her breasts, do you?" I actually whispered the word "breasts", because saying it out loud seemed so naughty. Not to mention it felt like a betrayal of sorts. I should not have been gossiping about my new friend's chest. But now I was curious.

Beth shrugged. "Everyone's doing it these days." Not much of an answer. "And anyway, shouldn't you be the one telling me? After all, you're bosom buddies now, aren't you?" She nudged me teasingly.

Telling her about the coffee rendezvous three weeks ago was such a bad idea. She'd been teasing me about "sucking up to the teacher" ever since.

"We had coffee after bumping into each other. Stop exaggerating."

Miss Petal looked our way, saw us and waved. I waved back, and through the corner of my eye saw Beth smirking.

"We both know that wave was just for you. Bosom buddies, see. I'd say Chester's got it made now. Those are the perks of being the son of his teacher's new best friend."

Beth went off to talk to one of the other parents, and not a moment too soon. It annoyed me that she thought I was using Ava to get special treatment for my son. She was so wrong.

"Chester, you need to tie your lace if you're going to be running around," I shouted, watching my son chase after his friends in a game of tag. An accident waiting to happen.

And then I waited. Not for the accident, but for what I'd grown to look forward to over the weeks. It usually took only a few moments for her to excuse herself, to ditch her male fans and make her way over to me.

"Good morning." She always wore the same, vibrant smile, as though she never had an off day and was always in a great mood.

"Ava, hi." And that was my usual response, as casual as I could manage, pretending that this brief interaction between us wasn't the highlight of my day.

"Did you have a good weekend?"

"So so. You? Oh, you went back home, didn't you?" She'd mentioned this last Friday when I'd picked up Chester.

"I did. Saw my parents. Had to listen to the usual moving back home speech."

"Parents!"

A few meters away Beth was watching us, grinning. She mouthed something that looked suspiciously like "bosom buddies", prompting me to look away. I was glad Ava's back was to her.

"Speaking of parents, I showed my mother some of your jewelry. She was very impressed. She thinks you're really talented."

"How nice of her to say." I had never been able to take compliments well; coming from her lips made them that much harder to endure. She had this way that she never took her eyes off me when she spoke, like she wanted to watch my reaction to her words.

"Well, it's true. Your work is amazing. I can imagine some big Hollywood starlet on the Oscars red carpet wearing one of your designs."

"Oh stop, you're just trying to flatter me." I laughed nervously.

"Take the compliment, Danielle, all right?" She put a hand on my arm. It was a friendly touch, but she took her hand away almost immediately, hurriedly, when I looked at it. She seemed embarrassed for doing it, and I hated that. Why the heck did I have to make her feel uncomfortable for touching me?

She cleared her throat. "Anyway, what I wanted to ask was if you would make a brooch for my mother. She's turning sixty, and I wanted to get her something she'll actually like. You do made-to-order, don't you?"

"Yes, of course. What does she like? Any particular theme or color scheme?"

"Butterflies. She's crazy about them. You think you could do something with that?"

"I'll get right on it. When do you need it by?"

She shrugged easily. "No rush. Her birthday's in a couple of months."

The first bell rang, warning everyone that they had five minutes to get to class before it commenced for the day.

"Well, that's me. We'll talk later, maybe?" she said.

"Sure. See you later." I watched her walk away, and the question that had been burning the tip of my tongue for weeks remained right where it was. I couldn't bring myself to ask, to even hint at it. For fear of rejection, of coming across as a freak. For a number of reasons, really. In my head I'd asked a thousand times, a hundred different ways. But when it came to it, I didn't have the balls.

On the walk home, once I'd ditched Beth at her house, I

gave myself a pep talk, insisting that this would be the afternoon I asked.

"I know you're still so new to town, and I have a couple of tickets to see a play by this local writer. One of my theater director clients gave them to me. I was just wondering if you wanted to come?" An old man walking past me shot me a dubious look and edged away from me a little, seeing me talking to myself.

The words were so simple. That was all it took, so what was I afraid of? The worst she could say was no. I had nothing to lose.

It took another two weeks for me to build up the courage to finally say it. At that point I'd almost run out of time. The play was moving on to another state, and only a couple of days remained. It was now or never.

"Oh, wow, my mother's going to love this!" She ran her fingers over the intricate sterling silver butterfly wings of the brooch. She was sitting behind her desk at the end of the school day, and class had already been dismissed. I'd told Chester to wait for me in the hallway.

"I almost don't want to hand it over." She laughed. "I guess I'll have to get one of my own. Thank you, really. How much do I owe you?" She opened the drawer of her desk and took out her purse.

"Nothing. It's fine."

"Absolutely not. You worked really hard on this. How much?"

"Ava, honestly it's fine. It's a gift. I won't accept your money."

She cocked her head to the side, and I imagined she did that to the children too. "That's not fair, Danielle. I can't accept it and give you nothing for your work. You don't have to do that."

"I know. I want to. Let's just say it's free publicity. Your mom wears it, her friends see it, and wallah, new buyers in Georgia."

It wasn't about the free advertising, but if I didn't say something she would reject my gift.

She put her purse down reluctantly, shook her head at me. "Thank you. You're very sweet. But how will you ever make any money if you give your stuff away?"

"I have a wealthy husband." I felt stupid for my joke, because the last thing I wanted her to think was that I wasn't independent. I made more than enough to support myself and Chester, if it ever came to it.

"Okay, well if you won't take my money, can I at least take you out for a drink? As a thank you?" She added the last line quickly.

I couldn't believe my ears. For weeks I'd been trying to ask her to the theater, and when I finally got the guts to do so, she sprung this on me.

Well, I'd spent far too long pumping myself up just to let it go now.

"Actually, I have a couple of tickets to a play in town, if you wanted to come? This Friday evening. I know it's short notice."

"A play? Sounds great. Drinks after?"

I could only nod, somewhat speechless. I'd expected a no, especially as it was so last minute. But a yes? And drinks! My heart was pounding so hard she must have been able to hear it.

Once we'd finalized the details, and I'd told her where to meet me, we said our goodbyes.

"Why are you always talking to Miss Petal?" Chester said when I met him in the corridor. He looked at me grumpily, and dragged his feet slightly as we started to the car.

"She's your teacher, love. It's my job to speak to her."

"You didn't speak to the others like that."

Observant kid. Too smart for his own good.

"Well, Miss Petal's nice." I'd used that word so many times to describe her that it had lost its meaning.

"Are you friends now?" This seemed to brighten him up.

"Get in the car, honey," was my reply. The safest one. Because I didn't know what we were, or what we were becoming. But when I thought about just being her friend, for a moment it didn't seem sufficient. And that frightened me.

SIX

Nothing in my closet seemed right for the occasion. Everything was either too plain or too formal. There was one outfit that would have worked perfectly...had I been able to fit into it. It was one of those "aspire to" dresses, you know the type you keep as an aspiration that you'll one day be the size you once were when it fit, so you could wear it again. For five years now it had been sitting there collecting dust...

"Goddammit!" I shoved everything aside. An hour to go before the big moment and I still didn't have anything to wear.

And when I realized I was doing this, freaking out because I didn't have the right outfit, my behavior baffled me. This was silly. Why was I acting like this was a first date? We were going to the theater and having a drink after – it wasn't some important, life-changing event that required me to be dressed to the nines.

But...it did matter to me. More than I could say.

And then I spotted it – the perfect outfit. A cream jumpsuit that I'd never worn, that I'd all but forgotten. There had never been a suitable occasion for it, and I'd never had the guts. Well, now was as good a time as any.

I climbed into it with ease, checked myself out in the mirror. No bulges, everything sat right. Even my breasts were given a lift, adding some perk to them. My stomach was relatively flat, thanks to all those abdominal muscle exercises. Not bad, not bad at all.

I gave myself an approving nod. Not a hair of my shoulder-length brown mane was out of place, and I'd taken my time with the mascara this time, avoiding the clumping and smudging that usually came.

Chester strolled into my room.

"Mom, where are you going?" he asked, sitting on my bed and watching me apply the rest of my makeup.

"To see a play."

"Are you going alone?"

I looked at him curiously. "No... With a friend. Why?"

"Erm, what friend?"

Now this was really getting strange.

"Honey, where's this coming from? Why all the questions?"

He looked at the door uncertainly, didn't know how to answer. And then I understood perfectly. Dominic. What a lousy jerk, using our son to extract information from me.

"You can tell your father that whoever I go to the theater with is none of his concern." I said it loud enough for him to hear, wherever he was.

He must have been standing outside the door, because five seconds later he stepped in.

"It is if you want me to babysit," he said.

"And there I was thinking you couldn't go any lower in my estimations, Dominic. Blackmail now, is it?"

"You're not the only one who has plans tonight."

"You said you would be home. You can't just change your plans last minute."

"Just reschedule. I'm sure your special friend will understand. What's his name anyway?"

I wanted to call him a piece of crap, to tell him to rot in hell, just hurl one insult after another, but my son was still in the room. So I simply shook my head in disbelief, but didn't respond. Keeping him guessing was delicious revenge. Two could play the game he'd been playing since we'd gotten together.

He looked at my reflection in the mirror. "Nice outfit. So this is the type of effort you make for someone who isn't your husband? Good to know."

This passive aggressive shit drove me nuts. He was always trying to play the victim. Never mind the fact that this was nothing but an innocent theater date between two women.

I ignored him.

"I didn't think you would want to wear something like that again. I mean, this isn't the pre-Chester years."

And when all else fails, try to lower my self-esteem so much that I don't want to leave the house. Whenever I went out without him this was his tactic. It had worked in the past, but he wouldn't succeed now.

It was time for me to spill the beans about my companion for the night. She was better than any male date because I knew he wanted to spend time with her.

"If you're lucky, Dominic, I'll share this little conversation we're having with Ava, when I meet up with her tonight."

I saw his reflection pale in the mirror. It was priceless.

"You're going out with Miss Petal? Since when?"

"Since a few days ago."

Now he looked at me with scorn, as though I was cock-blocking him or something. As though she belonged to him and I was depriving him of her.

"I will never understand why she would want to spend her time with you–"

"What, as opposed to you, you mean?"

"If you ask me the whole thing is weird. Two grown

women, at least ten years' age difference, teacher and mother of one of her students. It's freakin' strange."

I snorted a laugh. "Of course it is...when I'm the one doing it. Bet it wouldn't be so strange if you could take my place."

He narrowed his eyes at my back. I held back a laugh as I applied a dark cherry shade of lipstick.

"Well, like I said, I'm going out tonight."

"Fine, Lucy can watch Chester." I turned to my son. "How does that sound, honey?"

His face lit up with glee. "Yeah! I like Lucy."

What was not to like about a pretty, fun nineteen-year-old who gave lots of cuddles and let him stay up late? I suspected Chester had a thing for Lucy, the girl from a few doors down. And, sadly, he wasn't the only Thomas man with that affliction. My husband's whole persona changed when the girl was around. He tried to be as hip and carefree as he could, using words all the kids were using, but incorrectly. It didn't faze the creepy son of a bitch that, at forty, he was old enough to be her father.

My husband continued watching me apply my makeup, as though he wasn't aware that I could see him in the mirror. I wondered what he thought when he went silent like that. He did it often. A part of me, the hopeless romantic who hated quitting anything in life, wanted to believe that he was sorry for everything he'd put me through. That when he looked at me he realized what a fool he'd been for wrecking the only good and honest relationship he'd ever had. His parents loved me, his grandparents too. They all knew I was good for him...but he had never been good for me, and it had taken years for me to accept that.

He left shortly after, taking Chester with him and saying he would call Lucy himself. And I pushed all thoughts of him from my mind, replacing them with thoughts of my forthcoming evening with Ava.

I spotted her before she saw me, and it gave me the chance to admire her from a distance. She was standing at the magazine kiosk, engaged in conversation with a homeless man. She'd opted for a dress, simple and black, that didn't quite make it to her knees, and her fair hair was pulled into a loose ponytail. Her heels were twig thin; I wondered how she was able to keep her balance.

I was a little early because the taxi driver, a talkative, amiable Turkish man, insisted on speeding me to my destination, using the traffic lights and road signs as references only!

"But voting is important. A lot of people fought and died for the right to vote. I think we should all do it," she said to the man, who was ardently shaking his head.

"It's all nonsense. We have no power. Getting people to vote is how they control us, see?"

"You make a good point, but I still believe every vote counts more than you think it does."

I tapped her on the shoulder lightly, feeling bad for disturbing what was obviously a significant debate between her and her new friend.

"Hi. I can wait inside if you want to finish up here," I said.

"Hey." She looked surprised but pleased to see me. "You're early."

"So are you."

She laughed. "I have this fear of being late to everything, so I end up getting everywhere half an hour too early. It means a lot of waiting around."

"Ava, who's your friend?" the man said from among his filthy blankets and tattered clothes. His face was pleasant, like a toyshop owner's. But, wait a second. Did he just call her by her first name?

"Oh, where are my manners? Bernie, this is my friend Danielle. Danielle, this is Bernie."

"Uh, hello..." I gave him a wary wave, the unease likely visible on my face. I didn't feel comfortable with her giving my name to some random homeless guy, no matter how harmless he looked.

"We have to go now, Bernie. Gotta get to a show. You take care now." She shook his hand, then reached into her purse, pulled out a ten and handed it to him.

"God bless you, Ava."

"Wow, okay, so what was that all about?" I said as we made our way to the theater.

"I see him all the time. We discuss just about everything, from politics to music. He's a real sweetheart, very cultured. Used to be a professor of psychology, I think. Then the recession happened."

"That's awful. I wouldn't have guessed." I risked a brief look back at the man. A professor now unemployed and living on the streets? Bad luck could certainly happen to anyone.

"That was really nice of you to give him money."

She shrugged. "It's just money. Besides, he's the only friend I have here..." She turned and gave me a little smile. "Well, apart from you."

I gave her a goofy smile in response. So she *did* consider me a friend? She had no idea how much it meant to hear her say that.

"I love your outfit, by the way. Very chic," she commented, once we'd entered the theater and were waiting outside the doors to the auditorium.

"Oh, this old thing." I waved a hand dismissively, while blushing enormously. Any compliment, if it came from her, caused me to blush. And she was great at giving them. She always had something nice to say about me, I'd noticed that.

At school it was the same. If I felt like crap before seeing her, I felt a million bucks right after. And it was insane coming from this woman, who, by anybody's standards, made every other woman look like Quasimodo in comparison. If my outfit was nice, hers was incredible. If I smelled nice, she smelled delicious. If I was attractive, she was stunning. I should have felt like crap standing beside her, but she wouldn't let me. I'd been married for six years and Dominic had never made me feel even a fraction as good about myself as Ava did.

"And you look...beautiful as always."

If she hadn't been staring at me I would have made my cringe face then. How creepy did that sound? It wasn't the done thing to go around calling women beautiful, especially women you hardly knew. Why couldn't the show just start already?

"Thank you," she said. "So, is your husband babysitting tonight?"

"No, he's going out himself. Only decided that at the last minute. I think he wanted me to have to cancel my plans."

She frowned. "That's not very nice of him." There was something about her tone that made me think she wanted to say something else, something less polite.

"Well he's not a..." I stopped myself. He's not a very nice guy was what I wanted to say, but held back. This had been the closest I'd ever come to telling the truth about Dominic to another living soul, but I wasn't quite there yet. I wanted her, more than anyone else, to know my marriage was a sham, though I didn't know why. I felt like I could share anything with her.

Her eyes were soft and sympathetic when she looked at me. Pitying me. Then she rubbed my upper arm soothingly. "Well, you made it anyway, so boohoo to him. And we're gonna have a great night, just us girls. All right?"

It was already a great night just standing outside the auditorium. With her. And her touch, I could feel the hairs on my arm rising, and my skin tingling beneath my shawl.

SEVEN

Ava took one look at me when the curtain fell for the interval, and I knew, without her uttering a word, that she was thinking the same thing as me.

"So...that was a little graphic," I said, once we'd stepped into the bar for the fifteen minute break.

That was an understatement. It seemed like almost every other word was a profanity. But it wasn't just the swearing, the filthy sex talk made for a very unpleasant viewing experience. Perhaps if I'd been on my own it wouldn't have been so bad; but with Ava, I burned with shame. She must have wondered why I'd brought her to such a play.

She laughed. "On the plus side, my curse word vocabulary has been expanded ten-fold."

"Do you want to get out of here? I think we've seen all we need to see," I said.

"Yes!" She nodded heartily, and chuckling we left the theater.

We went to a bar a few doors down, a quiet place with mellow blues music playing in the background. She ordered a couple of cocktails.

"To us," I said, raising my glass and clinking it against hers. "And our new friendship."

"I'll drink to that."

I'd been nervous coming into the bar, knowing that it would be just the two of us, talking, delving into each other's lives. But once the alcohol started flowing, I relaxed.

"My husband thinks it's weird that I'm hanging out with you." By now my tongue was much looser, and my inhibitions on standby. I was in that happy, comfortable spot between sobriety and tipsiness, and planned to keep it that way.

"It doesn't matter what he thinks. Do *you* think it's weird?" She was leaning back easily in her seat, one slender leg crossed over the other. If my eyes had their way they would never be averted. It must have been the alcohol that was making me think like this, making me wonder how it would feel to touch those legs, how soft her skin was. Or how warm the inside of her thighs would be.

I cleared my throat, dragged my eyes away hurriedly, suddenly aware that the room was getting hotter.

"No, I don't. There's nothing wrong with people making new friends."

"Agreed. And so what if it's a little weird. I like spending time with you. A lot." She sipped what was left of her drink. Now it was her turn to look away.

"It's a nice night out. Do you maybe want to go for a walk along the canal?" I said, the idea just springing into my head. I don't know what made me suggest a walk, of all things. I hadn't gone for a pleasant stroll with anyone since a date in college. All I did know was that the drinks were finished, I didn't want another, but I definitely didn't want the night to end. Because that would have spelled goodbye for the whole weekend. I wanted to prolong this as long as possible.

"Sure. I was actually gonna suggest it myself."

She paid up, left a tip, then we headed out. There was only a slight breeze in the warm night air. Perfect weather for a stroll with a beautiful woman. An almost perfect night, if you discounted the atrocious play.

It was quiet on the streets and roads. We walked side by side, in-step, talking about nothing. Peaceful. I could have done this with her all night.

But then I switched gears. "Okay, I have to know. It's probably the burning question on everyone's minds at the school: why are you single?"

From the way her eyes grew wide, I knew my question alarmed her.

"I know it's very forward of me to ask–"

She nodded. "It *is* very forward."

"And you absolutely don't have to answer."

With the ample street-lighting I could see the little smirk that teased the corners of her mouth. "So we're getting personal now, are we, Dani?"

"Sorry, I know, it's none of my business. It's just that you're beautiful, and smart, and funny, and...God, the perfect woman. The perfect partner. And if someone like you is single, then the rest of us are doomed."

I could hear myself babbling but could do nothing to stop it. When had I progressed into solid tipsy state?

"And you said everyone at school wants to know this too?"

"The men at least."

Her smirk grew. "And you, of course."

"I mean, isn't there anyone you're interested in? Someone you want to get to know better?"

"Maybe." She smiled coyly.

"Okay, great, now we're getting somewhere." Although I played up the excitement, it was contrary to what I actually felt upon hearing that she was interested in someone. Why did I feel as though someone had punched me in the gut, twice?

Did I even want to hear about the punk who had stolen her heart? Probably some six-pack with jaw implants! Someone fake and plastic who would treat her like a trophy, ignoring the fact that she was amazing inside as well as out.

"Why are you so interested in my love life?" She chuckled.

"I don't know. Maybe because mine is so dire, I find it therapeutic focusing on other people's."

"You want to know why I'm still single? That right there, what you just said. I decided a long time ago that I would only date when I was sure I'd found someone truly special. Because I never want my love life to be dire. Real love, the kind that never dies or ages, retains the same potency throughout, no matter what. That's what I want."

My heart broke a little when I listened to her speak. Because I remembered the time when I'd been holding out for the same thing, been convinced I would find it if only I looked hard enough. And then Dominic came along, a wolf in sheep's clothing, promising me the world and giving me years of heartache instead.

"I hope you find what you're looking for." I meant that too. Just because my chance of eternal happiness was over, didn't mean I didn't want her to have that.

"I hope you do, too."

We stared at each other, stopped walking. Here we were, two women searching for exactly the same thing, but we couldn't give it to each other. I wished desperately that I could have been...I could have been the one she was waiting for...

As soon as the thought entered my mind, it spooked me. I turned away quickly, fearing that I would fall into those large blue eyes. It was crazy. And there was nothing to be gained thinking that way.

We started walking again. "You shouldn't wait forever, otherwise you'll have to keep fighting off all those hungry married men at school," I joked. "I mean, everyone's smitten with you. I can't really blame them. I kind of am myself. What do the kids call it these days, a girl crush?" I chuckled abashedly.

"You have a crush on me?" she teased. "I think you just said that."

I laughed hysterically, nervously. "Yeah, and I'm out of luck there, huh? I'm obviously not your type."

She stopped walking. Her face became serious.

"Actually, you are," she said. "You're exactly my type."

It all happened so fast. One minute she was looking at me, and the next her lips were on mine. So fast I didn't have enough time to decide what to do with my mouth.

And then it was over. She was staring at me, slightly horrified. Her expression a reflection of mine, it seemed.

I just gawked at her, my lips parted, slightly moist from her kiss.

"Oh my God, I'm sorry. I–I don't know what came over me. I'm sorry. Goodnight." She turned and hurried away, moving impossibly quickly for someone in heels.

"Ava," I called after her, but she didn't stop, didn't even glance back at me before jumping into a taxi.

EIGHT

It all made sense now.

Her lack of interest in the men around her, including Dominic, who was considered a catch by almost every woman in town. Her eagerness to spend time with me.

Dear God! How had I been so blind?

Lucy and Dominic were watching TV in the lounge when I walked in.

"Oh, Mrs. Thomas, you're back already." She sort of jumped up, her cheeks flushed, a guilty look in her eye. Had I just walked in on something?

"Yeah, we didn't expect you back so soon," Dominic said, a note of annoyance in his voice. "What's wrong, your new friend realized what a bore you are and left early?" He laughed cruelly to himself.

Demeaning me in front of the babysitter, what a classy guy. A real charmer. If this young, impressionable girl really fell for him, there was something wrong with the world. She was destined to repeat my mistakes.

But none of that bothered me. I was smiling on the inside. How wrong Dominic was about the reason for the date ending early. If only he knew. I still felt the memory of her lips against mine – soft and moist. The sweetest, most unassuming kiss. Whatever was happening in this room now, I couldn't have cared less about. Dominic could have been screwing the babysitter right in front of me for all the difference it would have made.

"How was Chester?" I asked.

"Fine. We had pizza, watched a movie, then he went to bed," Lucy said. She wasn't looking me in the eye, which told me everything I needed to know about what I'd almost walked in on.

Well, I wasn't about to pay her for making out with my husband. "Dominic, you can pay Lucy. Goodnight," I said and made my way upstairs.

I looked in on Chester before going to my own room. In the darkness I lay on my bed, still fully clothed. Then the smile that had been battling to come out sprung forth.

She kissed me! But that was only a small piece of it. I was the one she had feelings for, the one I'd envied, the one I didn't think would have been good enough for her. Not a muscle-bound man who wanted a trophy wife. Little old me. A *woman*.

It had never occurred to me that she might be gay. Through my ignorance I'd always imagined lesbians as women who wore their hair really short, and dressed in plaid and Doc Martens. Clearly I needed to get out more and not rely on TV depictions.

I ran my fingers over my lips. If I closed my eyes I could smell her, feel her. It was a memory I never wanted to forget.

But with the kiss followed the memory of her fleeing from me, and the horror in her face when she realized that by kissing me she had changed the nature of our relationship. What had she seen in my eyes that had made her run like that?

My smile faded. Why didn't I kiss her back, or at least say something instead of stand there like an idiot? Why didn't I run after her? Stop her and tell her it was...okay?

Was it okay, though? I still hadn't figured that out.

Lying in my darkened room, I ruminated over everything. Tried to understand how I felt about it. A married woman who, up until then, had thought she was completely straight. Had never thought of women sexually, beyond admiration for their beauty.

This was different. The truth was I'd been crushing on her in my own little way pretty much since I'd met her. A girl crush? No, how about just a plain old normal crush.

I was hot for teacher. And, judging by the kiss, teacher was hot for me too.

But now what? I didn't know if I was ready to deal with everything that came along with the revelation. Not least of all because I was still married; and still, for all intents and purposes, straight.

"Do anything special this weekend?" Beth said that Monday morning as we walked to school.

I hadn't said much the whole journey, my mind consumed with thoughts of seeing Ava again. I'd spent the whole weekend thinking about what I would say to her, but still hadn't come up with anything to convey my feelings. Mostly because I still wasn't sure what those were.

"Not really. I worked most of Saturday, and on Sunday took Chester swimming and to the park. Standard stuff."

"Believe me, I would have killed for standard. It was the weekend from hell for me."

As soon as she launched into telling me why are weekend was so bad, I zoned out, my own worries plaguing my thoughts the nearer we got to school.

The gates came into view, and panic set in. Just a minute to go and we would be face to face again. My throat was as dry as sand.

The kids ran ahead, as usual.

"Hey, Miss Petal really is something, isn't she?"

The mention of her name threw me. I gawked at Beth.

"W–what do you mean?"

"You know how Jack was having problems with multiplication? I'm seeing a big improvement. And in his spelling. Miracle worker. I'm not the only person saying it, either. If she can straighten my kid out, I don't care if my husband wants to sleep with her!" She chortled to herself.

The "miracle worker" was the first person I saw when I stepped through the gates. As usual, she was engaged in conversation with one of the fathers. These routine exchanges I had once looked upon with irritation and a hint of the green-eyed monster. Now I saw things differently. Now I knew better.

I waited for her to see me, to come over. And when she finally did look my way, instead of wrapping up her conversation and joining me, she continued speaking with the man. It was as though I wasn't even there.

Maybe that was for the best anyway, despite it making me feel like crap. What would we say to each other now, with all these people around? We could talk later, I decided. And by then hopefully I would have something worth saying.

The children filtered out of the classroom as the final bell of the day sounded throughout the building. Home time. I was already waiting in the playground with Miranda and another mom I spoke to on occasion.

With the bell went my nerves. It was time to confront her.

"Do you mind just watching Chester for a couple of minutes? I need to have a little chat with his teacher," I said to Miranda when I spotted Chester walking out of the building, his backpack almost half the size of him.

I said a brief hello, ruffled his hair as I passed, and told him to wait with Miranda.

I sucked in a deep breath, steadied my nerves as best I could, then plodded along the corridor to her room.

The door was wide open, but I knocked it anyway. She was sitting behind her desk, looking through a stack of papers, so serene, like an angel. She looked up, saw me and froze for a moment.

"I hope I'm not bothering you," I said.

"Actually, I'm pretty busy–"

"I think we should talk," I broke in.

She stood up, pretended to busy herself with the things on her desk, doing everything to avoid looking at me.

"That's unnecessary."

"How can you say that after...well, you know."

She laughed humorlessly. "You can't even say it."

It wasn't that I couldn't, but that I didn't want to. Not here, not with the door wide open, where anyone could hear. It was between us, this beautiful thing that had happened, and I wasn't ready for the whole world to know about it. Not yet, before I even knew what it meant myself.

"Ava, please, I don't want to make this awkward."

"Okay, and we won't. It was a silly mistake, a misjudging of the situation. It won't happen again, Danielle. You have my word." She collected some papers into her arms. "Now, if you'd excuse me, I have a meeting to get to."

"Ava," I said, but she was already walking past me to the door, barely looking at me.

My fingers ached to restrain her; my tongue burned to say the words that would stop her. But I couldn't. Not just because I was afraid, but because I genuinely didn't know what the right words were. Perhaps I should have told her the one thing I was certain of: I wanted it to happen again. And again. And again...

To say she was cold with me over the days that followed wouldn't have been accurate. It wasn't exactly a coldness, but a distance. She treated me almost as politely as she did everyone else. And I hated it! Our morning and afternoon conversations about any and everything had ceased. Even the polite smile of greeting she gave me had nothing in it. Being treated like everyone else sucked!

It went on like that for two weeks, as awkward as I suspected it would be; and once they were gone, I soon realized just how much our little talks had meant to me.

It was Friday afternoon, an hour before I had to pick up Chester from school, and I was vacuuming the lounge. Smash, smash went the cleaner into the furniture, as I furiously worked. I'd been cleaning the house since noon, not because it was dirty, but because it soothed me to clean. Well, it usually did. Today was the exception.

Everything infuriated me! The couch, the coffee table, the homemade lamp we'd had flown in especially (and expensively) from Italy. The weekend was about to start and I'd fallen into a funk. A funk that had been building for two weeks, and had finally come to a head.

So she kisses me and then decides I'm not worth talking to anymore, I thought bitterly. *Who does she think she is, huh? Where does she get off?*

The vacuum cleaner cut out suddenly. I spun round furiously to see Dominic standing with the wire dangling from his hand.

"What the hell did you do that for?"

"Your phone's ringing," he said. He handed it to me. "Beth."

I didn't want to speak to her, but he'd already answered for me. I glared at him. He'd no doubt been poking through my phone, reading my messages, seeing who I'd been calling lately. He'd done it before and made no secret of it.

"Beth, hi."

She spoke quickly, said she and her husband were stuck out of town and wouldn't make it back in time to pick up Jack, and if I could get him.

"Geez, what bit you in the ass today?" Dominic said once I'd hung up. "You walk around like that too much and your face will stay that way." It infuriated me more when he was in high spirits. I think he fed off my bad mood, like a mood-leech or something.

"It's no small wonder I don't already look like this permanently, living under the same roof as you," I snapped.

He only laughed, and I immediately regretted showing my anger, because I knew it only encouraged him to torment me.

"You're welcome to leave any time. Going back to your parents and confessing that your marriage has failed, after all the bridges you burned with them when you married me? I don't think anyone's going to be waiting with open arms."

It wasn't as awful as that, though I had become somewhat estranged from my parents. They hadn't even turned up to the wedding. My brother and sister, thankfully, were still in contact, however infrequent.

"How did you ever get like this?" I asked, shaking my head in wonderment at the man I'd wasted almost a decade of my life with.

He cupped my chin in his hand. "Honey, I have always been like this. You were just too in love to see it."

I batted his hand away. His touch made my skin crawl half the time.

"It's a good thing I don't have that problem anymore."

He laughed again. "Have you found someone new? Is that

it? That's why you're finally taking pride in your appearance again. Come to think of it, it started when that sexy little blonde started working at Chester's school."

My glare deepened. I tried not to show a flicker of recognition when he spoke about Ava.

"A little competition is always a good thing."

I snorted a laugh. "Competition. Do you want to know something? That little blonde, no matter how much you insult me or go sniffing around her, will never be interested in you." It was on the tip of my tongue to tell him the reason why, and to take infinite pleasure in also letting him know that I was the one she wanted. But I kept my mouth shut.

I dropped the vacuum cleaner hose, left it where it was in the middle of the room, and started off.

"Well, I already told her that our marriage is as good as over, so we'll see how long it takes," he shouted after me.

I heard, loud and clear, but I didn't stop on my way up the stairs.

The son of a bitch! He told a complete stranger something like that? How long had she known? Before the kiss?

Once I got over the initial rage of what he'd done, I was able to see the funny side of it. So there he was trying to show that he was available. But what he'd really done, unbeknown to him, was shown that *I*, the person she actually wanted, was available! Oh, the irony.

I left home early, not wishing to be under the same roof as Dominic. But mostly because I wanted to go for a quick drive before collecting the boys, before seeing her again.

I parked the car, took the deepest breath I'd ever taken, and strode through the school gates like a woman on a mission, head held high. Even though I was shaking like a leaf in a storm, I wasn't about to chicken out.

"Hey boys," I said to Chester and Jack when they and the rest of their class came out a few minutes later, accompanied by their teacher. She made the briefest eye contact with me, and then went back inside once all the kids were with their parents or guardians.

Both boys were in high spirits because Jack was coming home with us. For some reason unknown to me my house was the mecca of fun. Dominic, despite his flaws, was actually pretty good entertainment for the kids, when he was around. That might have been it.

"I need to speak to Miss Petal before we go." I didn't want to leave them in the playground, so I brought them along, told them to wait for me in the corridor where I could still see them.

Just like before, the classroom door was open. But unlike the last time, I didn't knock. Her back was to me as she wiped the board clean. Her golden hair was slightly messy, and her red cardigan had bits of glitter on it, much like Chester and Jack.

I closed the door behind me, and she spun round, startled.

"Danielle...I mean, Mrs. Thomas."

The correction bugged me. Why were we back to formal speech?

"Don't do that, Ava. It's not fair." My tone came off more agitated than I'd planned.

She frowned. "Do what?"

"This. Everything. I'm not going to do this anymore. I said I didn't want this to get awkward." I slowly made my way toward her, each step causing her to look more and more unnerved. So now she was afraid of me?

"We don't have to do anything. You're the one insisting on bringing it up. I just want to forget the whole sorry episode." She looked away, distressed.

This wasn't how I had envisioned our talk going. I hadn't come here to unsettle her.

Now only the desk stood between us. But not for long.

"Really? You want to forget about it?" I said, walking around the piece of wood that separated us, until I was standing right in front of her. "So you're ashamed of kissing me? You regret it that much?"

"That's not what I me–"

My lips were on hers suddenly, cutting her sentence short.

Jesus Christ, I was kissing her! Kissing a woman! And...and no kiss had ever felt so right. I'd kissed dozens of men in my life, and none of them had ever felt this natural.

I held her head in my hands, comfortable in my dominant role. It took a couple of seconds before she opened her mouth and let my tongue in. And then it suddenly became a tango of tongues.

When a kiss is good, really good, it can feel as though it's lasting an eternity. But this one, unfortunately, had to come to an end. I broke away first, remembering where we were and who was waiting for me outside. Getting caught playing tonsil hockey with my son's teacher wasn't something I wanted.

She just gawked back at me, eyes wide with shock, lips puffy and wet, lipstick smudged. All my doing, and I felt great about causing it.

"Now we're even," I said, and started to the door. I stopped with my hand on the knob, looked back. "And I don't regret a second of it."

I left her there the way she'd left me by the canal – flabbergasted, speechless, unable to comprehend what had just happened, and what it meant.

"Why are you smiling, Mom?" Chester asked when I rejoined them. Thank God he hadn't seen us.

"Because it's a good day, honey. And it's been a long time

since Mommy's felt this happy."

I realized that I'd probably confused the situation even more by doing what I'd just done, but I didn't care. I'd taken a walk on the wild side, kissed a woman and loved every moment of it.

NINE

So where did we go from here?

That was the burning question on my mind, and likely on hers. What would the next move be, and who would make it? Although I wanted to believe the ball was in her court, being the married one, the one with a family, and presumably the only one who was new to same-sex relationships, the responsibility fell on me to okay it.

Whatever *it* was.

The weekend was more agonizing than it ever had been. Each spare moment I had, I closed myself in my bedroom, brought her number up on my screen, and battled with the urge to hit call. Like a smitten teenager in high school, who had managed to snag the hottest girl in school's number.

I even wrote up a pros and cons list for calling. That was how much thought went into my decision. The cons, however, outweighed the pros, and by Sunday evening I still hadn't made it. The following day would be Monday; whatever we had to say could be said then.

It was just before six in the evening, and we were in the middle of dinner.

"The potatoes needed more salt," Dominic said, tucking into his meal regardless. There wasn't a meal I prepared that he didn't have something negative to say about. The vegetables were too soft, the meat was too well-done, or too rare, or too whatever. If he wasn't complaining he wasn't happy.

I cut him a look. "You know how to ensure someone else doesn't ruin your meal? Make it yourself," I said. I had to be careful with how I spoke to him around Chester. Telling him that he was an ungrateful piece of crap who was lucky I still cooked for him probably wasn't suitable for the sensitive ears of our seven-year-old.

"Don't get so defensive. A little constructive criticism improves us all."

I wanted to slap the grin off his face. My handsome husband who, since making his jerk act a permanent feature in our marriage, had become the ugliest person I'd ever met. It was funny how that happened.

My phone's lively ring jingled from the living room. Usually we didn't take calls at dinner, but Dominic's face was especially irritating to me that evening, and I wasn't hungry. I left the room to answer it, ending the charade of our happy family act.

I froze when I saw the caller I.D.

"Hello," I said, making my way quietly up the stairs. Her merely calling me, post-kiss, put us in dangerous territory. Because now the call meant something entirely different, something far less innocent.

"Hi." She sounded uncertain.

Just hearing her voice set my heart racing. I closed my bedroom door behind me, sat on my bed. "I'm glad you called."

"Are you?"

"Yes. One of us had to. We need to talk," I said, and bit my lower lip.

"Talk, you mean like we did on Friday afternoon?" There was amusement in her voice.

"Well, I did come to talk, but...I guess I seized an opportunity."

"To kiss me?" She laughed. I relaxed.

"Just returning the favor."

"So you haven't run to your priest, prayed for absolution yet?"

I chuckled. "Not yet. I'm thinking maybe I should try it a couple more times before I do that."

"With someone in particular, or would anyone do?" That singsong southern accent now took on a smooth, sultry tone that sent a shiver down my spine. All of a sudden this had become real. A real same-sex attraction. Real flirting. Real arousal.

"I have someone in mind..." I said.

Maybe she heard the uncertainty in my voice – no, not uncertainty, just nerves – because her tone changed.

"Look, the last thing I want is to make you uncomfortable, Danielle. I know this is a difficult situation."

"It is, but not because of you." I wanted her to know that, despite how inopportune this all seemed, she wasn't to blame. Feelings didn't give a damn about marriages and families and gender. If someone had told me that prior to meeting Ava, I wouldn't have believed a word. Now, I got it.

"But it is. I never should have kissed you. You're married. I don't want to be a home-wrecker."

"There would need to be a home to wreck," I mumbled to myself. "I don't know if you should be throwing words like that out there. We're friends, and we had a moment. A couple of moments. Maybe we should just let the chips fall as and where they may."

"What does that mean?"

What *did* it mean? "I like talking to you, spending time with you. We should do that. Nothing immoral about that, is there?"

"No, I think that would be nice."

I could just imagine her smile, and wished I could have seen it. I never got tired of seeing it.

"Good. So that's settled."

We spoke like true friends for another fifteen minutes, never bringing up the kiss or anything associated with it. Neither of us dared admit the obvious elephant in the room: that there was nothing moral or innocent about what we wanted to do to each other.

When I pulled my door open, Dominic was waiting outside, pretending that he hadn't just been listening. I wondered how long he'd been out there, and how much he'd heard.

"Is there a problem?" I asked.

"No. Why?"

"What are you doing outside my room?"

"It's my house, Danielle, I can go wherever I want."

I rolled my eyes and stepped past him to go down the stairs. "Grow up."

"Who was so important to talk to that you missed dinner with your family?"

"That's none of your concern."

"You're my wife. Don't you think I have a right to know what you do?"

I laughed, out of shock more than anything else. "Wow, really? This is not the nineteenth century, Dominic. And I'm your wife in name only."

"If you're seeing another man, Dani, I swear to God..."

He glowered at me, more angry than I'd seen him in a long time. His voice was raised too.

I stared at him, mouth agape – all I could do at the obvious double standards. This jerk had been screwing every woman that walked past him, rubbing it in my face to boot, and yet he had the audacity to condemn me for *possibly* doing it.

I returned to my son in the kitchen, keeping shtum about the fact that I wasn't seeing another man. Another woman, however... And if I had anything to do with it, we would be doing a lot more than simply seeing each other.

TEN

It had been so long since I'd dated, that I'd forgotten all about that exciting new relationship buzz you feel at the start.

Anticipating texts. Calling to say goodnight so that her voice was the last thing you heard before retiring to bed. The dates to places you'd visited many times, but that were made novel and special simply because she was with you. I'd forgotten it all.

The problem with this, however, was the fact that we seemed to be doing all of it as friends. It was as though she'd taken my words literally, that platonic friendship was all I wanted. Because we didn't kiss again over the following weeks. We didn't even hold hands. Plenty of opportunities arose for it – strolls through the park, a boat ride along the river, sitting in a darkened movie theater right at the back, where no one could see us. And every time I thought she was about to lean in and kiss me, she turned away, moved on to something else.

My biggest fear had been realized: we'd become best friends!

Six weeks passed like this, and the closest I came to intimacy with her was the goodbye hugs and pecks on the cheek. And something inexplicable started happening to me after every one of our rendezvouses: I was growing more and more frustrated. Frustrated with myself for not being forward, taking the lead and instigating another kiss. Frustrated with her for being so damn beautiful, and tempting, and inadvertently teasing me.

I didn't recognize myself when I got into one of my moods. This crippling desire to be with another person was new to me. It no longer fazed me that she was a woman, that she was younger, that there were a hundred things that made her unsuitable for me.

It was the last day of the semester, and I'd gone to pick Chester up. When the bell sounded, she escorted her class out of the building as usual, and said her hellos to the parents. It didn't take long for her to join me, her smile always so huge and inviting. A little while ago I'd thought that it grew a little wider just for me, but lately I wasn't so sure. Lately I'd been questioning her true intentions, and if they'd changed now that she'd gotten to know me better.

"Hi there," she said, her eyes twinkling somewhat mischievously. Oh, why did she have to be so irresistible? It only exacerbated my frustration at being stuck in the friend zone. What a miserable place to be.

"Hey," I said a little weakly.

She always smelled like candy, super-sweet and totally bad for my health. And I wanted every inch of her!

"So have you decided whether or not you're going away for the holidays?" she said.

I shook my head. "Maybe for a few days in the second week. I have a couple of friends who live in Toronto. I was thinking of taking Chester there. They have a little boy his age."

"Sounds like fun. I've never been to Toronto. Canadians hate me, for some reason." She chuckled.

"I can't imagine why anyone would hate you," I said. "When do you leave for Bolivia?"

"Mid-week. I wish you were coming."

She'd proposed it a couple of weeks ago, during one of our many non-romantic dates. It was as if she'd forgotten that I had commitments, had a kid to look after. I would have followed her to the moon if I wasn't tied down. And even though I loved my son more than anything, the ceaseless burden of being a mother did sometimes way down on me.

"We could take Chester with us, you know. He would love it out there. It would also give him a chance to learn some Spanish."

The three of us, a happy family, out there in rural Bolivia. I would stay at home while she went to teach English to the school kids. The image put a smile on my face, but reality wiped it away promptly thereafter.

"I couldn't, you know that."

"Yeah, I do." She looked genuinely disappointed. "It's going to be hard not seeing you for almost two weeks."

I laughed. "You'll forget about me the minute your plane lands. Maybe even sooner." But I would be thinking about her every second of every day, eagerly awaiting her return, praying that she didn't enjoy it too much out there and never come back.

"That's not true." Her eyes were sincere when she said it. If she would have kissed me right there, right then, in front of everyone, I wouldn't have minded. Why hadn't she tried again? Could everyone see the way we were looking at each other? I often wondered if anyone could see what lay between us simply by observing the way we stared at each other.

"So listen, you remember I told you about the book club I joined, and you said you wanted to come along? Monday is my turn to host."

Book clubs had never been my thing, not least of all because I'd never met anyone interesting who belonged to one. Until Ava. She was odd in her hobbies. Like, for instance, her adoration for manga. She'd even attended a couple of Comic Cons. "I'm a nerd at heart," she'd once said. A beautiful nerd. I imagine I wasn't the only one who found her a bit of an enigma.

"Monday? At your place?" I asked. It would mark my first visit inside her house.

"Yes. 7PM. Do you still want to come?"

"Sure, why not?" I wasn't coming for the others, and not even for the books. I was coming for her. And if I wouldn't see her for ten days, I had to get as much time in with her as I could before she left.

I regretted the blouse as soon as I stepped into the car, but it was too late to turn back and change. The tag itched like hell, and I was afraid to tear it off in case the shirt ripped.

A bottle of Burgundy lay on the passenger seat. I wanted to get there early so we had some time alone. But when she opened the door, and the lively chatter spilled out, I knew my plan had been foiled.

"Hey, come on in. Almost everyone's here." She kissed me on the cheek, took the bottle from me, and ushered me in, missing my disappointment completely.

She introduced me around the room of eight strangers. They sat in her living room, clutching coffee or wine in one hand, the book of the week in the other. With the exception of two young men, whose age I put at early twenties, the people in the room had an overwhelming similarity: over forties, glasses, and presumably an account at the same outdated clothing store in town. They were exactly as I'd pictured them. And within five minutes of sitting down, dispensing with niceties and smalltalk, it became clear to me why the two young men had come here. In that we shared a common goal: Ava.

"Did you get a chance to read the book, Danielle?" she asked.

"Half of it. I couldn't finish the rest." It was a thriller about a man who hitchhiked across Europe, and the discrimination he faced because of his race.

And so the evening kicked off. I stayed quiet through most of it, trying to keep myself awake, or trying to ignore the blatant flirting the two boys were doing with Ava. Outrageous to the point of being nauseating.

When the older folks were talking, I busied myself looking discreetly around the living room, marveling at Ava's quirky style. The drapes, the rug, the paintings all seemed to be African in design – at a guess, West African. Little wooden safari animals took pride of place along the mantelpiece. She sure had a thing for Africa.

But it was hard to focus on the furnishings when two horny men were firing off just about every lame line in the flirting manual, and doing so in the sleaziest, most unsubtle manner.

"Ava, no one would drive past you if you were hitchhiking."

And, "Did you say you're a teacher? Those kids are so lucky to have you as a teacher. I would never miss a day of school."

And worse still, "I liked the book. It was a love story. A lot of men my age don't like to show their sensitive side, but this really touched me. You know what I mean, Ava?"

I almost threw up in my mouth at that last line! Couldn't they hear themselves?

The night, thankfully, came to an end just before nine. The older folks said their goodbyes and promptly left.

"It's still so early, Ava. What are you doing now? Did you

want to come out with us?" one of the boys said. Besides me they were the last to leave. They were lingering, and it was so blatant.

"Jesus," I mumbled to myself. It came out louder than intended, and Ava looked at me, somewhat amused.

"Thanks, guys, but I'm a little tired. Got a lot to do tomorrow, you know. Maybe some other time."

Why couldn't she just tell them she wasn't interested, that she was gay? Why did she always have to be so damn polite?

I collected my things up just as they did, and we all made our way to the door. So much for our alone time.

"Danielle, you said you'd take a look at my computer for me, remember?" she said quickly, once we were all in the hallway.

"Did I?" I frowned. I couldn't remember saying anything of the sort, and didn't think I ever would, because computers hated me.

"Yes, remember? That thing wouldn't start and you said you could fix it?"

"We can take a look at it for you," one of the boys jumped in, any excuse to stick around. I doubt they knew any more about computers than I did.

"That's okay, Danielle said she would do it. See you guys in a few weeks." She opened the door and all but shoved them out, smiling the whole time.

The penny, as they say, finally fell.

She turned to me, smiling, shaking her head. "Well, you didn't make that easy for me."

I laughed, feeling foolish. "God, I'm so sorry. Stupid. I heard computers and it completely threw me. I thought you'd gone senile."

She chuckled as we returned to the living room. "I had to think of something. They do this every week."

"How do you put up with it?"

She shrugged. "Guys have been doing that from the moment I hit puberty and grew breasts! I've learned to ignore it mostly."

She had the patience of a saint. Even *I* wanted to punch them. But that might have had something to do with my wholly unreasonable jealousy, the type that had been rearing its ugly head since Ava walked into my life. It wasn't an emotion I had a right to when it came to her, particularly as I could no longer muster any when it came to my own husband.

"So just to be clear, you don't have a computer you need me to take a look at?"

"No computer. Just a bottle of Burgundy we our name on it."

She went to fetch the bottle and some clean glasses while I made myself comfortable on her couch. No more annoying hangers-on, no more books, just the two of us. Alone. We'd been alone several times, but not like this. Always in public. Never unrestricted.

We chatted for an hour while we enjoyed the bottle I'd brought. It never took much to get me tipsy; and together with the natural high I was already on just being alone with her, I had reached saturation point halfway through my second glass.

We were sitting beside each other, and had been the whole time, but only now, with the alcohol running through my veins, and my senses amplified, did it really start to affect me.

"This goddamn tag has been bothering me all night. It's a new top."

"I hate when that happens. I have a pair of scissors in a drawer somewhere if you want to cut it out?"

She got up to fetch them, disappeared from the room. *Screw the blouse!* I thought, unbuttoning it. If I accidentally cut it, too bad. I didn't care anymore. My back was sore.

When she walked back into the room, scissors in hand, I was already shirtless. Normally I wouldn't have even considered removing my shirt like that in someone's living room. I guess I was more tipsy than I'd first thought. Not to the point that I didn't know what I was doing, simply enough to allay my inhibitions. My insecurities about my body had also been alleviated.

She handed me the scissors, almost expressionless. She didn't sit back down beside me, just stood on the other side of the room by the window, watching me cut the tag out of my shirt.

"It's pretty hot in here. Maybe I'll keep my blouse off," I said. It was a joke, and in a way my attempt at flirting. I wanted to see how she would respond, because her need to be so far away from me seemed odd.

"If you like. It's up to you." Now she was doing her best not to look at me. Something was definitely up. Did she want me to leave?

"This is my first trip to your place and I end up topless. If this is how all book clubs end, I'm sad I missed them all those years," I continued.

She didn't laugh, only offered me a little smile that faded almost as soon as it came. It was as though she was now bored with me and couldn't bear to hear my voice, or even look at me. Wow, was I really that grotesque?

"Is everything all right?" I asked, putting my blouse back on. The sight of me was obviously making her uncomfortable.

"Of course. Why do you ask?"

"Because you've gone really quiet."

"I'm just thinking, that's all."

"About what?"

She shrugged. "Stuff."

"What sort of stuff?"

"I don't know, Dani. Just stuff." She seemed agitated now. And that set me off.

"You're not being very hospitable right now, I hope you know that," I said, furiously doing up my buttons.

"What?" She looked at me, perplexed.

"You heard me. If you want me to go, you should just say so, all right."

"Why would you think I want you to leave?"

"Because of your body language. Maybe you would prefer those two boys as company instead of me." I didn't know what had come over me, or where those words had originated from. I was now too annoyed to care that I may have crossed a line.

And I was on a roll. "Why did you bother going through that whole charade of getting me to stay if you were going to ignore me?" I wasn't letting her get a word in edgeways.

I leaped up from my seat. "I think it's best I go now. I don't want to make you any more uncomfortable than I already have."

She called my name but I ignored her on my way to the door. But fury still flowed through my veins and bones, and before I knew it I'd turned back into the living room.

"No, I have a few things I need to get off my chest first. And then I'll leave." I slammed my purse down on the couch. She stared at me as though I was a madwoman and she didn't know how I'd gotten into her house.

"It's not fair what you're doing, you know. Spending all this time with me, strutting around all perfect and beautiful, and sexy. So damn sexy!"

She cleared her throat, and I thought I saw the makings of a smile teasing her lips.

"And every moment that we're together I'm battling the urge to kiss you, or touch you, and it's the hardest thing I've ever had to do, keeping my hands off you when you're sitting right there."

I took a breath, and she carried on watching, silently. Yep, it was definitely a little smile, more visible now.

I continued, "And I have to come to terms with the fact that now that you've gotten to know me, you're no longer attracted to me... And what the hell is so funny?" I demanded, upon hearing her laugh.

"I'm sorry. Are you done?"

I couldn't believe I'd just poured my heart out and her response was to laugh at me.

"You're something, you know that, Dani? I think we'll have to keep you away from the wine in future. It makes you delusional."

"I'm not delusional," I said defiantly.

"Oh, but you are. You think that I'm not attracted to you. I'd say that's as delusional as it gets. I've done everything I could these past few weeks to spend as much time as possible with you. I call you half an hour after I've just seen you. Heck, I wanted you to come with me to Bolivia, and you still think I'm not interested in you."

She walked toward me slowly. "See, completely and utterly delusional." She brushed some strands of hair out of my face, her eyes soft, her smile tender.

I swallowed. "But what about before? You couldn't even look at me. I was sitting on your couch half-naked."

"Oh sweetie, that wasn't because I didn't want to look at you, it's because I *did* want to. Believe me, I know quite a bit about having difficulty keeping my hands to myself when I'm around you. I didn't want to make you uncomfortable."

Uncomfortable? Wasn't she aware that every moment spent

in her company, as her "friend", was the real agony? I'd never experienced anything like it. It was as though my body had been pining for her, crying out for her. To convey that to her would have been impossible without sounding like some sort of pervert.

I shivered slightly from her touch. I stared into those sapphire-like eyes, losing myself in them. She looked uncertain. Whatever she saw in me made her hesitant.

"I want you to know something," I said, taking the hand that she'd used to brush my hair away. "I didn't come here for the books." I pressed my lips to the back of her hand. Without the alcohol in my system I probably wouldn't have made a move like that. It had always seemed so cheesy when others did it. But she smiled.

"I didn't set out to fall for a married woman. I don't want to break up a happy home."

"I haven't been happy in years. Truly happy, maybe never." Who knew whether or not that was true? But in that moment, the only happiness I could remember was being with her. I couldn't think of one good thing, beside Chester, that had ever come out of my marriage (and even he had been conceived before we married).

We were still holding hands, but she gripped tighter, and the next thing I knew I was being led out of the living room. I followed silently, my heartbeat speeding up.

We climbed the stairs, neither of us speaking. Words were unnecessary now; this short journey upstairs said everything.

Her bedroom was decorated the way I'd imagined it: light, airy colors, all the furniture, including the bed, foreign. African was my guess. I made a note to ask her about the African thing when this was over.

It was a huge, sturdy-looking bed made of finely carved mahogany. Upon seeing it, I started to panic.

Holy shit, this was really happening! In a moment she would expect me to perform, to do things I'd never even considered before I'd met her.

All the confidence I'd started out with had deserted me now, and I stood in the middle of the room feeling like a lamb to the slaughter. There were two conflicting positions battling inside me. The first – fear of the new experience. And the second – exhilaration at finally doing something my body had been craving for months.

When she leaned forward and kissed me, however, I immediately felt more at ease. It was a simple kiss that reassured me.

I gave as good as I got, letting my tongue loose in her mouth. Before long the kisses ceased being polite, and we attacked each other with so much force, so much beastly passion, that we fell onto the bed.

Perfect timing, because soon kisses simply weren't enough. I had no idea what I was doing, what was expected of me, but none of that mattered. Whatever my role was, I wanted to get into it pronto.

As such, I was the first to reach for her clothes, pulling at them while she was on top of me and we were still lip-locked. I kept thinking that any minute now she would stop me, because something this wonderful, with someone so amazing, couldn't possibly happen to me. But she didn't.

"Are you sure this is what you want?" she asked, once she came up for air, having detached her lips from mine.

I nodded and pulled her into another kiss, using it as an opportunity to unbutton her top.

She laughed as we kissed, but it faded shortly after when passion took over. And when we separated again, I was able to relieve her of her top altogether.

I ran my hands along her smooth body. Across her midriff,

over her breasts, which were tucked away in a fancy, pale green bra. I touched her while she watched me, my first time doing something like this – admiring and desiring another woman's body.

Beth's words came to mind then, as I caressed Ava's bosom. And a smile came to my lips.

Beth, I can confirm, and with pleasure, that they are one hundred percent the real deal. And I'm going to enjoy every mouthful!

She did the honors, reaching back and undoing her bra slowly. It was like waiting for my lottery numbers to be called!

I took in a deep breath, now faced with the two mounds. They were so perfect I was almost afraid to touch them. Almost, but not quite. My mouth watered.

I ran my hands over them again, and goosebumps spread across my skin when I felt her nipples harden against my palms.

I sat up, pulling her close and into a kiss, her nipples pressing against my chest. But as nice as that felt, there was only one place I wanted them.

I ripped my mouth away from hers, and trailed kisses along her jaw, then along her neck, taking my time, sucking and licking every part of her flesh, not wanting to leave any untouched.

She breathed gently, letting out the tiniest moans each time my lips pressed against her.

And then I arrived at her mounds, kissing around one before taking it into my mouth and suckling on her teat. Now her moans were far more audible. I sucked hungrily before moving onto the next breast. I was an unstoppable machine, switching back and forth, hungrier and hungrier for the sensation against my tongue. Hungrier still for her breathless moans. These alone could have made me climax, I thought.

I wanted to go on forever, and couldn't believe how naturally something like this had come to me. It felt as though I'd been doing this sort of thing for decades, as though women were the only lovers I'd ever known.

But I felt her pulling away. At first I thought that through my enthusiasm I'd hurt her. But she kissed me, and started undoing my blouse. She wanted us to move on. It was my turn now.

Once my blouse and bra were off, she pounced on my loose breasts, skipping the build up. She abused my mounds with her mouth – her lips and tongue worked together to send me into a delirious state. My breasts had never been handled this way before, and I couldn't get enough of it.

"Oh, that's beautiful," I whined, my eyes shut tight.

"You're beautiful," she whispered while she suckled.

When she was done, she kissed her way back up and found my lips again, her blonde tresses falling over my face and curtaining us.

"Are you still with me?" she asked, stroking my face.

"Of course." Despite the lingering fear of the unknown, and of my inexperience, there was no place I would have rather been. Nothing else I wanted to do. And no one else I wanted to be with but her.

"Good," she whispered, kissed me again before descending. It was her way of preparing me for what would come next, I realized that later. Because foreplay was one thing, but she had more in store for me.

I trembled when she started working my jeans off, and trembled even more when she slipped her fingers into my panties.

"It's all right, sweetie," she said softly, our lips reuniting again. The kiss was a way to distract me while she penetrated me. I loved the feel of her nipples rubbing on my chest, of her stomach on mine, while her finger swam through my soaking canal.

She sank a couple of fingers inside me, and watched me unblinkingly as they made their passage. She wanted to see the effects of her move. My eyelids fluttered, the feel of her inside and out, at the same time, incredible.

I moaned against her lips as she brushed them across mine.

"Do you like how I feel inside you?" she breathed, sex in her voice.

"Yes," I croaked, nodding. I kept nodding as she glided in and out of me. "Yes."

"And what about if I touch you here, would you like that too?" She already had, on my nub, which the penetration had made sensitive to the touch.

She was barely kissing me, teasing me with the promise of a kiss. Likewise down below, her fingers stroking only lightly, but just enough to get me writhing.

I couldn't answer with words, just a moan of consent. I felt so powerless beneath her, even though we'd started out as equals.

Then she kissed me, and at the same time commenced her strumming on my swollen bean.

I wanted to focus on kissing her, but I was too busy moaning and wailing.

"Oh, Ava, Ava." Over and over. Her name was perfect for calling out during sex. It just rolled off the tongue. I also loved screaming it. It made me proud to do so, proud to be the one privileged enough to be with her. If the dads at the school could have seen me... If Dominic could have seen me.

"I've wanted to do this to you since I walked into the classroom that first evening," she said. "I thought about this more times than I would like to admit."

"Don't stop," I said in response. She'd been going for several glorious minutes. Her fingers must have been tired, given the force and speed at which she moved. But I couldn't bear the thought of her depriving me of this wonderful sensation. Selfish, I know, but it had been a long time since I'd had sex, and even longer since I'd enjoyed it, and I didn't want this to end.

She carried on for several more minutes, per my request. Eventually she did stop. I hadn't reached my peak, and she'd built me up so much that I had real fear she was too tired to finish.

I realized I was mistaken when she started taking her pants off. Within a few seconds she was buck naked, and her attention went right back to me, back to my remaining piece of clothing: my panties, which she dragged off frantically.

She spread my legs open and bore down on my sex with her mouth.

What followed I knew, no matter what became of us, I would remember forever. Remember the way it felt the moment her tongue first connected with my bean, after swimming through every corner of my sex. Remember the way I moaned and whimpered incessantly.

I thrashed about like a fish out of water, almost broke free from her hold of my thighs.

She never stopped sucking, licking, and stroking my nub with her tongue, slurping me up like I was a sweet beverage. Nor my cries of ecstasy nor my violent writhing stopped her. Only when I expired, trembling as the spasms tore through me, did she let up.

I hadn't survived very long, I knew that much. She'd worked me up too much beforehand, and her tongue had been relentless in its assault on my bean. I didn't stand a chance. I came screaming her name... The best way to climax.

I felt like I'd been exorcised, rid of a demon, at the end of it. I lay there on her bed, spent, hardly any energy left to even keep my eyes open to look at her when she came up to meet me.

"Hey," she said. Her lips were moist with my sap. She licked it off while I watched her, and I let out a tired laugh. "Yummy."

"I hope I wasn't too much of an amateur for you," I said as she stroked my face lovingly.

"You were great. I knew you would be."

ELEVEN

"You know you have exactly the same body parts as I do?" She giggled but didn't move, didn't push my hand away.

We lay in her bed facing each other, the bed sheet only coming up to our thighs. My fingers had been slowly caressing all the grooves and curves of her body – her breasts, her stomach, her thighs – for several minutes. I didn't think I would ever tire of touching her.

"They're better on you," I said.

"I don't think so. I love them on you, Mrs. Thomas." She arched closer and kissed me. That was another thing that would never get old. When she kissed me I felt like all the bad in the world disappeared.

We'd been like this for an hour or more, I'd lost track of time. Not saying much, just happy touching and kissing.

"What's put that smile on your face?" she asked.

"You, of course. I'm happy." It was such a simple thing to say but it meant so much, more than she would ever know. Saying it only made me realize how unhappy I'd been all those years. It had taken one night – albeit an amazing, mind-blowing one – with a woman to show me that.

"So am I."

"You were happy before you met me though. That's the difference."

"I was *content* before I met you. What I'm feeling now, that's something else." She sounded so sure, so convinced of this, that I didn't want to argue with her. But her constantly happy persona was one of the things that attracted me to her...along with everything else, of course. She was like a breath of fresh air in my miserable, mundane life. Getting through another day living under the same roof as Dominic was made infinitely easier knowing that I would get to see her.

"I hope I'm not dreaming," I said, still tracing my fingers along her flesh. I loved looking at her naked form; perfect in every way, but mostly because I got to enjoy it, and I continued to enjoy it.

"You're not dreaming," she whispered. "This is real. We're real."

I didn't know what that last bit meant, but it made me smile to hear it.

But I knew it all had to come to an end. Because there was another reality that I had to get back to: my son, my marriage, my home.

I intertwined my fingers with hers. She smiled back at me. It had been a long time since someone had looked at me like that.

"It's so late already. I'll have to leave soon."

"I know. You have a life to get back to. I hate letting you go."

This honesty was so new to me. She didn't feel the need to hold back, suppress her true feelings. Was it always this easy to be open with female lovers? I'd been missing out big style.

"I don't feel good about going."

"I wish you were coming with me to Bolivia."

"I can't, Ava."

"I know. Will you promise me one thing?"

I was ready to promise her anything, no matter what it was. Those blue eyes made me want to do her bidding.

"What?"

"Will you think about me while I'm away?"

I gave a little laugh. "Every day." Didn't she know I would be unable to think of little else? Almost two weeks with the memory of our love-making. The wait for her return would be agonizing.

"These are going to be the longest two weeks of my life." I hesitated for a moment before I said my next line, aware how awful it would sound if it came out wrong. But we were being so honest, I wanted her to know exactly how I felt. "Please don't hate me for saying this, but I'm kind of hoping you hate it out there so you don't stay there for good. I have this fear that once you get there, you won't want to come back. With all those beautiful Latina women walking around you..."

She laughed, and without asking climbed on top of me. It was amazing how used to the feel of a naked woman between my thighs, against my flesh, I had gotten; but more surprising still, how much I craved that feeling. She was so soft, her touches so gentle.

She peppered my face with light kisses. "Why on earth would you think that?"

"Because I'm too happy, and I don't think it will last." I had to swallow back the tears that were threatening to erupt from me, tears I hadn't realized I'd been holding in. I didn't know whether I was tearful due to my happiness, or the thought of losing it.

"What has he done to you?" she said, her face registering her ire. "He's made you think you don't deserve to be happy."

She kissed me, kissed all my pain away, and said nothing more about Dominic.

"I'm coming back, I promise. There's so much to come back

for."

I hoped I was one of those things.

"And while I'm gone," she started, pinning my arms down and sinking her chest lower onto mine so that our breasts met, "I want you to think about all the naughty things you want me to do to you when I return."

I giggled giddily as she kissed my face and neck. "That's a given."

The kisses inevitably led her down south once more, where she gobbled up my sex all over again, this orgasm much more paralyzing than the last. I didn't leave her house until three in the morning, and grinned all the way home in the car.

I tried to make as little noise as possible when I let myself in that morning, and crept upstairs in darkness. I started across the landing to my room when I heard giggling and whispering coming from Dominic's room. Two voices, one distinctly female.

I froze in my tracks, a cold sensation spreading over my body.

In our house, while our son was sleeping! And knowing I would be home eventually. He'd gone too far. He truly was a scumbag of the highest order. Disrespectful, tactless, vile.

My blood boiled while I stood there. It was all part of his game to be as disrespectful as he could, in his goal to hurt me. Whatever remaining respect I had for him disappeared that night, never to be seen again.

The woman of choice didn't matter. Nor did the length and extent of their affair. As far as I was concerned, he could stick his disgusting manhood in anything, as long as he kept it away from me and our family. Up until then he'd managed to adhere to that. My being out so late, on what he assumed was a date, must have really eaten at him. Driven him crazy to imagine his wife with another man. He probably had built an image in his head of what this tall, dark and handsome stranger looked like, just as I used to when his affairs bothered me.

That was the thought that settled me that night, stopped me storming into his room and exposing them both – him and his current whore of choice. In my outrage I'd almost forgotten the amazing night I'd just had, with the most amazing human being I'd met in a long time.

I carried on to my room, calmed down. What did I care that he was so blatantly screwing another woman in our home? Who was really coming out ahead between the two of us? Whatever he had with these other women would never be as pure or real as what Ava and I shared.

As I lay down to sleep that night, my body still tingled from her touch. It was magical. When I shut my eyes I could remember the intense way she looked at me as we made love. It wasn't merely slotting pieces in and only caring about her own release. No, she was a considerate lover, taking her time, making sure that we connected on multiple levels. The sort of sex I could only have dreamed of.

Except, she wasn't a dream. She was one hundred percent real, and she wanted me just as much as I wanted her.

Dominic came out of the bathroom just as I was going in. It was just after seven, and I'd been woken by my hyperactive son bounding into my room and demanding his breakfast.

"I didn't hear you come in last night," my husband said.

I rolled my eyes. "No? What about the woman in your bed? Did she hear me?" Of course he'd heard. He'd probably prompted her to laugh especially so that I could hear.

His poker face needed work. "There you go again, Danielle, making things up. What must it look like in that head of yours?"

"Whatever, Dominic." I went in and slammed the door in his face, because it looked as though he wanted to come in with me. Those days were long gone.

But he was still hovering outside when I finished.

I sighed heavily. "Don't you have anything better to do? Some stocks to buy? Women to hound?"

He laughed. "I don't hound women. If anything it's the other way around. I mean, come on, you should know better than anyone how it goes. You stalked me for months until I knocked you up and you forced me to marry you."

I narrowed my eyes at him. If looks could kill the slimy worm would have been dead years ago. This wasn't the first time he'd said something like this, and I was sure it wouldn't be the last. He liked to remind me, whilst embellishing, that I had been the one to pursue him. But I resented his making it out that I'd somehow tricked him into getting me pregnant, and marrying me. Yes, I'd been foolish, naive, head over heels in love with a bad boy, having convinced myself I would be the one to change him. So many women had, my story wasn't unique. But he'd taken advantage of my naivety. It had given me my son, and for that I would always be grateful, but it didn't change the fact that I'd screwed up.

And now I was suffering heavily for it. Though that suffering, thanks to Ava's entry into my life, had been made all the more bearable.

"Just get out of my way," I said, shoving past him.

"Who were you with? That teacher again?"

"What's it to you?"

"I don't know if I'm comfortable with you spending so much time with her. I don't want her putting any ideas into your head. This coming home late nonsense, when you have a young son. She's obviously a bad influence on you. I might have to have a word with her."

"Don't you dare! What I do with her has nothing to do with you," I hissed. I could have clawed his eyes out. So typical, trying to take away this wonderful thing from me.

He laughed wickedly. "Wow, you need this friendship more than I thought. You know that once she's found friends her own age, hot young women who haven't started going gray, and whose bodies aren't forever tarnished by childbirth, she'll ditch you, don't you?"

He always knew how to get to me. Knew all the right buttons to push in order to sink my confidence into the ground.

"You're the worst human being I've ever met," I said to him and dashed to my room. My attempts at suppressing the tears were in vain, and they dropped quietly while I tried to regain my composure.

It was all so ridiculous. Okay, so my body wasn't as svelte as it once was, but it was in no way disgusting. And the gray hair he'd spoken of, I'd found only a couple, that was it. No big deal. I knew all of this deep down, yet I still let him get to me. Only a few hours earlier I'd been in bed with a woman who'd told me I was beautiful all night, and had kissed me everywhere, touched me everywhere, and wanted more. I should have known better.

It would take time to get him completely out of my head. Something I had to work on. Something Ava would help me with.

I just had to survive the next two weeks.

TWELVE

Her text came in just before eleven the Sunday before the new semester was set to start. But I saw it the Monday morning, when I woke up to get Chester ready for school.

Ten days without a word from her had been tough. I'd known beforehand that she was going to be living out of cellphone range, in the hills in South America, but it didn't make it any less frustrating.

So the arrival of her message brought relief and joy. Relief because it meant she was back on North American soil. Joy because it meant I was still on her mind.

She'd stuck to her promise and returned. None of it had been a lie. Her message said she missed me, that she was counting down the hours until she saw me again. I'd worried for nothing, having convinced myself that I would never see her again. That maybe her plane would go down over the Andes. Or any number of things that would keep us apart forever.

Chester and I met up with Beth on the way to school that morning. Beth looked the worse for wear.

"I'm glad that vacation is over and that the little demon has gone back to school. I thought it would never happen!"

"Was Oklahoma really that bad? You usually love it out

there," I asked. Her parents had moved out there four years ago, sold up one day and bought a place by the lake.

"Jack was a little shit all week! I don't know what got into him. It didn't help that my parents spoiled him rotten, gave him everything he asked for, even after I told them not to," she groaned. "I thought about leaving him on the highway multiple times on the drive back."

I chuckled. "That's not a very motherly thing to say."

"Ach, what do you know? Your son's an angel."

I certainly had been blessed. Although Chester did have his little tantrums, he was a well-behaved kid, mature and polite ninety-five percent of the time. The other five percent I attributed to his father's genes dominating.

"But enough about me. You're in high spirits today. Relieved to be getting your days back, huh?"

"That too," I said, a coy smile settling on my face. I'd been smiling like that ever since reading Ava's text.

Beth gave me an intrigued look. "Oh? What aren't you telling me? What's got you grinning like that?"

"Gosh, you sound just as bad as Dominic. Can't I smile because it's good to be alive?"

"No, I know you, Danielle. Something's going on with you. You've been like this for a while. Whatever it is, I could do with some myself."

I laughed. The cause of my elation was something I didn't ever want to share. And somehow I didn't think Beth would have gone for it anyway. Well, four months ago I wouldn't have imagined myself sleeping with a woman. Now I couldn't imagine *not* doing it!

A nauseous feeling swirled in my stomach – the type of pang you get when you're about to go on stage in front of a bunch of people. But this was more nervous excitement than simple nervousness. It started as we approached the school gates.

My eyes scanned the crowded playground, expecting to see her among the parents. But she was nowhere. I left Beth and the kids in the playground, and headed inside to find her. I couldn't wait any longer to see her; I'd just about survived ten days.

There were still ten minutes till school started. The classroom door was closed, but I saw her through the window. The blood rushed to my head.

"Come in," she called when I tapped the door.

Moment of truth.

She was fixing the books in the reading corner, and when she turned around, her face lit up. God, she was more beautiful than ever. Maybe because I'd missed her so much. But I think it had something to do with the new tan she now sported. Golden, sun-kissed skin complemented her blonde hair perfectly. She looked as Hollywood as it got, except there was no airbrushing here.

It was all I could do not to run up to her and kiss her. My mind went racing back to the last time I'd seen her, how naked she'd been, and all the things we'd done together. It almost seemed wrong to think about them in the classroom, but I couldn't help it.

"Hey," she said. "I was hoping you would come find me."

"You look great." Now that we were reunited, I didn't know what to say. I knew exactly what I wanted to do, however.

She made her way to me until only a few feet separated us. Any less than that and it would have looked suspicious if anyone were to walk in. "I missed you."

"I missed you too." I held back from telling her never to leave again, because that would have been coming on too strong. Heck, we'd only spent one night together. Getting attached this quickly wasn't healthy. "How was your trip?"

"Very unglamorous and tiring. So, in other words, amazing! I can't wait to go back. They've invited me back in summer."

"For the whole summer?" I asked, unable to hide the worry in my voice. I'd barely managed a week and a half. What would I do for six?

"Yeah. Maybe you should think about coming with me this time."

"That sounds a lot like blackmail to me," I joked.

She laughed. "Perhaps it is." Then she touched my hand with the back of hers, her fingers stroking mine as discreetly as she could manage. "I really missed you," she said again.

The touch was everything. We were like forbidden lovers, like something out of a 1950's film.

"I want to kiss you," I said.

"It's killing me to see you right now and not be able to do that...and more."

I felt my cheeks heat up. It didn't matter that I'd been thinking the same thing, hearing her say it made it all real.

"I know you're probably jet-lagged and want to rest tonight—"

"No, I want to see you," she jumped in before I could finish. She squeezed my hand. "I want to see you every night."

I couldn't believe this was happening. Someone who wanted me as much as I wanted her, and who wasn't afraid to make it known. Had I walked into an alternate universe where I got everything I ever wanted all the time? It sure felt that way.

"Will you come this evening? Just for a couple of hours if that's all you can manage?"

I didn't even need to think about it. "Yes."

The door opened then and our hands quickly separated. One of the fathers, come to do his routine flirting, oblivious to the fact that he was not only barking up the wrong tree, but was in the wrong forest entirely!

I said goodbye to her then left the room, grinning from ear to ear. He could flirt outrageously till the cows came home, but I was still the one she wanted.

"Did you brush your teeth, honey?" I asked Chester, when I came to tuck him in that evening.

He nodded, and when I sat on his bed, he provided the proof by breathing his minty breath in my face. I chuckled, ruffled his hair, then tucked him in.

"You look nice, Mom," he said, yawning, his eyes heavy.

"Thank you, baby. Always such a gentleman." He certainly didn't get that from his father.

"Are you going out?"

"I am. To see Miss Petal."

"Why?"

"Because she's my friend, and I want to hear all about her trip to Bolivia." Among other things.

"Are you going to her house?"

"I think so." Where was this questioning going?

"Can I come?"

I laughed, kissed him on the cheek. "Not tonight, honey. Maybe another time, if Miss Petal is all right with that." I watched him yawn again, barely able to keep his eyes open. "But I think you've had enough for one day. Goodnight, sweet dreams."

I switched off the light, and bumped into Dominic on my way out of Chester's room. He was like a pimple – unwanted, infuriating, hard to get rid of.

"So yet another night you're spending out with that woman? What exactly is it that you do together?" I heard the insinuation in his voice, and it frightened me. He wasn't stupid; sooner or later he would join the dots.

I decided not to fuel the speculation and said, "We do what women do, sit around bitching about how worthless the men in our lives are. What else?" *Yeah, you wish!* He was hardly even a passing thought, and certainly the last thing on my mind, when she was inside me, when her tongue was down my throat. If he knew how little he mattered when Ava and I were together, it would have depressed him.

"She'll get bored soon, Danielle. Everyone does with you, I should know."

"So you keep saying. Goodnight, Dominic." I laughed to myself. Nope, he couldn't get to me no matter how hard he tried. Not tonight. Tonight was about Ava and me. I was mere minutes away from making love to a beautiful woman again; none of the junk that he spewed could hurt me.

The second her door closed, I pounced on her like a tigress devouring a deer. Up against the wall, I kissed her hungrily, skipping the hellos. I could say hello any time; this was far more important.

And inevitably, the kissing, for me at least, didn't suffice. I tore her clothes off frantically, right there in the hallway, and she did nothing to stop me.

I stripped her down to her panties, frilly, expensive-looking things. Pretty, but right then simply an obstruction.

I kissed down her body, gobbling at her breasts the way I had before. But they were just a stop on my ultimate destination. And the panties had to go.

I slid them down her thighs, not taking my time. I sank to my knees as she stepped out of the thong and kicked it away. I put one leg over my shoulder and buried my face in her crotch. Her scent drove me wild. She smelled like paradise, and I imagined she tasted that way too. Time to find out.

I had no idea what I was doing, but did what I liked myself.

I also utilized some of her own moves, the ones she'd used on me. She was already wet. I didn't know how long she'd been like that, or if that was my doing. But I lapped up her sap, maneuvering my tongue all around her sex, bottom to top, top to bottom, side to side. Leaving no area untouched. That was more for my enjoyment than hers, as her taste, as predicted, was delicious and addictive. Far better than the male equivalent, which I had never liked. This I could eat for supper, every night, for the rest of my life.

She moaned a little while I worked, her hand touching my head lightly. "That's it, sweetie."

Hearing her moan because of my tongue made me proud. Encouraged me to go ahead. I hit her bean next, and kept hitting, striking with my tongue, doing gymnastics against it.

Her new, louder whimpers coincided with the assault. Her grip on my hair tightened. I felt her fingers digging into my scalp. If someone walked past her house they would have surely heard her, and probably me too, lapping away like a thirsty animal to water.

I knew that she'd climaxed because I felt the tremble against my mouth, and her final whine was louder, deeper and lasted longer than the rest.

"You weren't lying when you said you missed me too," she said with a breathless laugh.

"Sorry, I just really needed to do that."

She took me to bed after, and we drank wine.

"Are we going to have to talk about what this is at some point?" I said. We were sitting up in the bed, naked, me in her arms.

She kissed at my neck and the side of my face. "I thought it was pretty clear what this is," she whispered against my cheek.

Her breath tickled, and I giggled. "What is it?"

"Two women who can't get enough of each other. Wouldn't you agree?"

"Yes...but...can anything ever be that simple?"

"I suppose not. But we could make it as simple as possible."

"How can it be if I have a husband?" I wanted her to tell me to leave him, to force me into action in order for our affair to continue. It was unreasonable to expect that request from her so early on in our relationship. Our second time together, hardly enough of a preview to be sure she wanted more from me than a few rolls in the hay.

"I don't like that this is the only way to be with you, and it will be difficult to look your husband in the eye from now on, but...well, Mrs. Thomas, you're just too damn irresistible."

I kissed her, and when that one ended, I kissed her again. I had never been, and didn't know I could ever be, irresistible to anyone. The self-confidence my husband had spent years trying to insult out of me had been officially restored by her.

"Does he know where you are?"

"Yes, he overheard me telling Chester. I think he was insinuating something, about us. Or maybe I was being paranoid."

"He won't come to that conclusion, don't worry. Men never do. They think they're imperative to our happiness, and can't really fathom a world in which they don't factor. He probably thinks we're doing each other's makeup or something!"

I burst into a laugh. "At nine in the night? Yeah right."

She didn't laugh though, and when I turned to look at her, she looked slightly agitated. "What's wrong?"

"I don't want to laugh about it. I feel bad. I respect the sanctity of marriage, I really do, and–"

I kissed her, cutting her off. "My husband has been cheating on me since we started dating. In fact, he was still seeing his ex-girlfriend when I fell pregnant with Chester. Two wrongs don't make a right, I know that, but it's a bit too late for anyone to gain a conscience in this marriage."

She looked like she wanted to say something, but she didn't, just smiled sadly. "He probably doesn't deserve you, but I still don't like sleeping with someone else's wife."

It annoyed me that she saw me as that. It ruined the paradise I was trying to maintain, where here, with her, was the only place Dominic didn't feature.

"I know he spoke to you about our marriage a while back," I said. "Told you we were as good as done."

She looked away. "That was just because he…"

"You can say it. It doesn't bother me. He wanted to get into your pants. Wanted to convince you that you weren't breaking up a happy home if you slept with him. Well, he wasn't lying. We haven't slept together in almost two years."

"If that really is true, why do you stay together?" The million dollar question.

"Convenience. Chester." I shrugged. Terrible reasons to stay in an unhappy marriage. "I don't know. But you have to know that it isn't for love. It hasn't been about that for a long time."

She wanted to say something else, but yet again kept it to herself and just wrapped her arms around me tighter.

"Let's not talk about him anymore," I said.

"Deal."

THIRTEEN

"Mom, can I take this too?" Chester jumped up and down beside me, holding up a Frisbee.

"Honey, you already have the bucket, the spade, the football and the kite. How many things do you think you'll have time to play with there?" I chuckled as I loaded the food into the cooler bag. Sandwiches, fruit, jello, cookies, chips, soda... It was as if I'd packed for a month in a bunker instead of a few hours at the beach!

"But I *need* this," he said. He obviously thought that adding stress on the word "need" would get him whatever he wanted. I wasn't convinced that taking a Frisbee with us was a matter of grave urgency.

"You need oxygen to breathe, honey, but you don't need the Frisbee."

"Please. Pretty please."

"Fine! All right, you can bring it. But that's the last thing. We have to get going in a minute."

I was in a giving in mood. It was a pleasant Sunday, and we were about to have a family day on the beach. At least, my idea of a family day.

Dominic pulled into the driveway as Chester and I were leaving. He hadn't come home the night before, and was still wearing yesterday's clothes. You can probably guess how little I cared about that.

"Hey, champ. Where are you off to?" he said, giving Chester a playful punch to the stomach.

"We're going to the beach," Chester said excitedly. "I'm gonna build the biggest sand castle ever, with a moat and everything. And right beside it I'm going to build pyramids, like they have in Egypt."

"Sounds like fun. Why wasn't I invited?" He said it to Chester, but I knew it was directed at me.

"Because I want to enjoy the day," I muttered.

"You can come, Dad. Then you can help me."

"No, he can't," I broke in quickly. "He's busy. Get in the car, Chester."

Dominic looked as though he wanted to argue, wanted to make my life that much harder by tagging along. I prayed he didn't insist on coming, because that would have been dire. The family day I had in mind didn't include him.

"Another time, bud. I've got a lot to do today."

Chester slumped into the passenger seat dejectedly. "You always have a lot to do."

I didn't want to feel bad for depriving them of time together, but nevertheless the guilt hit me as I strapped myself in. Dominic had all the time in the world to spend with his son, but he chose to sleep around instead. I shouldn't have felt bad.

"And there I thought you only ever went out these days with your new bosom buddy," Dominic said, leaning through the driver's seat window as I started the engine.

I pressed the button to close the window, and he quickly jumped away before he got trapped in it.

"Real mature, Danielle," he grumbled as I pulled out of the driveway.

I spotted her immediately when the car pulled to a stop in the parking lot. She was standing by her car, big shades on, sarong wrapped around her torso. Her hair was tied up. I grinned to myself when I looked at her. Men and women of all ages strolled by on their way to the beach, marveling at her flawless beauty. She paid no attention, just kept her head buried in her magazine. Without seeing I knew it was a manga comic. She had piles of them at her house. Hoarded them, by her own admission.

She looked like an incongruous joke someone was playing on the whole beach: this beautiful woman, more stunning than a supermodel, reading a comic, and paying no one any attention.

But I knew better. This was the woman I'd been spending my evenings with for the past three months. My lover and best friend.

"There's Miss Petal, Mom," Chester shouted, pointing excitedly. I hadn't informed him that she would be joining us. And I was glad, too. He would have told Dominic, and Dominic, in turn, knowing that he could destroy the day for me, would have insisted on coming.

"Is she waiting for us?"

"She might be," I said coyly.

He unbuckled himself hastily, in a hurry to get to the woman he saw five days a week, several hours a day. He spent more time with her than I did, yet he still wanted more. I certainly knew how that felt.

"Well hello there, you two," she said when she looked up and saw us.

"Hi Miss Petal," Chester said in that singsong voice all kids seem to have when they address their teachers.

"What have you got there? Is someone going to make a

sandcastle today?"

He nodded shyly. He got like this around her still. It was hilarious. My son was crushing on my girlfriend!

She bent down to his level. "Can I let you in on a secret? I love building sandcastles. Do you think maybe we can pool our resources and build one together, to make the biggest, baddest sandcastle anyone has ever seen?"

He nodded emphatically, grinning. He didn't know what pooling one's resources entailed, but I guessed he would have gone along with anything she said. She spoke like that to her pupils often, using big words and foreign words to enrich minds.

"I thought I would surprise him, so I didn't tell him that you were coming," I said as we made our way down to the beach to find a good spot. Surprisingly it wasn't nearly as full as I'd expected. Likely because the sun wasn't out, though there was a sweltering heat.

Chester chased his ball, playing a one-man game of soccer. As Ava and I walked, our arms rubbed. I needed that contact, however fleeting and innocent it was.

"I so want to hold your hand right now," she whispered.

It was always agony to be out with her in public, hence why most of the time we stayed at her place, away from prying eyes.

"And I'm fighting the urge to kiss you," I whispered back. No one would have batted an eyelid if she had been Dominic, a man I despised but still a man all the same. It wasn't fair that I couldn't show my affection for her in public.

We found a spot not too far from the sea, and set down our blanket and baskets. Ava and I didn't get a chance to speak much, because Chester pulled her back up and demanded that she make good on her promise to build a super sandcastle with him.

"Chester, let Miss Petal have a rest before you put her to work," I pleaded.

"It's fine," she laughed. And they were off.

I could have gone home and left the two of them there. That was how much I was ignored while they amused themselves. When they realized that their super sandcastle wasn't working out, they abandoned it and set off for the sea instead.

"Is this really happening to me? I'm actually in competition with my son for your attention?" I joked, as Ava stripped off her sarong and prepared to catch up with Chester. Although she'd dressed appropriately – a top and shorts swimsuit combo – and I'd seen her far more naked than this, her body always stunned me.

"'Fraid so, sweetie. Sorry."

"You're going to have some serious making up to do later."

She laughed. "I can't wait." It would have been the optimum time to lock lips, but as it were, no kiss came.

I rested back on my elbow and watched them frolic in the sea. I'd never been so happy. And I'd never felt like a family unit more than I did then. The perfect image: two parents who didn't hate each other, a son they both adored, and who loved them back.

I laughed as they splashed each other. She was such a big kid when it came to Chester, but more mature than I'd been at her age when we were alone. I still couldn't believe how seamlessly we all fit together.

"Dani, is that you?"

I spun around, startled, and saw Miranda, her husband and daughter approaching.

"Great," I muttered under my breath. What perfect timing. Not! Of all the days to come to the beach, they had to pick today.

"Hi guys." I forced a smile. "I guess you had the same idea."

She set up her blanket right beside mine.

"Look, Mama, Miss Petal is playing with Chester in the sea," Emma pointed out, and I cringed a little.

Miranda squinted in the distance. "You're right, Em', it *is* Miss Petal. You came here together?" She turned to me with a curious expression.

I shrugged. "She was going and I thought it might be good if we tagged along, that's all."

"Hmm." She grinned mischievously. "You sure ditched us, didn't you? For a younger model. We're not good enough for you now that sexy Miss Mississippi is on the scene?"

I didn't bother telling her that Ava was from Savannah, Georgia, and not from Mississippi. To her, the Deep South only consisted of that one place.

"It's not like that at all," I said miserably.

"For God's sake, Fred, pull your tongue in! Have you never seen a woman in a swimsuit before?" Miranda snapped at her husband, who hadn't taken his eyes off Ava since discovering she was here.

"Don't be so crude, Miranda," he grumbled, embarrassed, his cheeks turning red.

They settled down, and their daughter eventually joined Chester and Ava in the sea.

"It's actually really good having our children's teacher as a friend. It's like having a babysitter on tap," Miranda commented, lounging back and watching the three of them splashing around. "And Emma loves Miss Petal. Maybe I should go everywhere with her too. Could be an investment in my daughter's future."

This bothered me more than it should have, her intimating that my friendship with Ava was tactical. Beth had said something similar.

"I'm not friends with her for any reason other than that

she's a really nice person, and we have a lot in common." I hated having to defend myself. Her ogling husband would have annoyed me more if I hadn't been used to most men gawking at Ava like that. It went with the territory of dating a beautiful woman. And even before Ava, it had happened with Dominic. Would I ever learn my lesson about dating great-looking people?

"Hi Miss Petal," Miranda said when Ava joined us, soaking wet all over. "Good to see you."

"You too, Mrs. Hawthorne." She reached for her towel and dried herself off, unaware that she had an admirer, and it wasn't me. Miranda's husband was having a hard time keeping his eyes off her. I didn't blame him.

Unfortunately Miranda did, and noticed immediately. "Go play the kids," she ordered.

Knowing that he'd screwed up, he didn't dare disobey.

"Men are disgusting sometimes!" she said, making a face. "Sorry for that, Miss Petal."

"For what?" Ava asked, completely oblivious. She settled down beside me, but made sure to keep some distance between us.

"Just my husband being a pervert."

"Oh." Ava shot me a cringing look, which I responded to with a clueless shrug.

"I keep telling him, whenever he brings you up, that you'll never be interested in him. That chances are you like your men with more hair on their heads, and less stomach." She cackled to herself and didn't see me and Ava exchange another look.

She doesn't like men, period, I fought back the urge to say.

"I think he's just being polite," Ava said.

"Unlikely. He's into you. They all are. Sorry if it makes you uncomfortable me saying that, but it's true. Isn't that right,

Dani?"

I cleared my throat. "I'm not sure it's really an appropriate topic of conversation–"

"Oh relax, would you. Miss Petal's one of us now. We can tell her these things. I bet you girls talk about this stuff all the time when you meet up on your special little dates."

I knew Miranda, and I knew that she wasn't implying anything close to what was actually happening, but it still made me uneasy. I also wanted to save Ava from this. I loved Miranda and all, but she was as coarse as they came, unapologetic with it, and had no filter. I had a feeling that the day was on its way to becoming even more awkward for both me and Ava.

"The water's really nice, Dani. You should go for a quick swim," Ava said. I heard the desperation in her voice for a change of subject.

"Are you seeing anyone right now? Everyone's just eager to know. It would also stop a lot of the hounding at school if they knew that you were taken," Miranda continued. She'd never been able to take a hint.

Through the corner of my eye I saw Ava smirking. "My love life isn't nearly as interesting as people think it is."

Miranda sat up, intrigued. "Oh? What does that mean?"

"Well, it's all very simple. I am seeing someone, and I'm happy." She looked at me quickly, then added, "Very happy, in fact."

Miranda, thankfully, didn't notice a thing, because the look we exchanged was so telling. Ava might as well have just outright blurted the name of her lover to the whole beach.

But, her confession touched me. We'd said it to each other several times, that we were happy, but hearing her admit it to another person really brought it home.

"Ha! See, I told you, Fred, she's taken and very happy.

Tough luck!" Miranda shouted to her husband, who was currently being buried in the sand by his daughter and Chester.

Miranda had made it her goal, it seemed, to embarrass him at every opportunity. I wondered how they'd stayed together so long. I certainly couldn't have been married to her for a day, let alone fifteen years.

He ignored her, looked away grumpily. I wasn't sure whether that was because of the news about Ava's relationship status, or because his wife was demeaning him in public.

"Dominic didn't want to come?" she went on, looking at me.

"Uh, no, he was busy." *And wasn't invited.*

How many awkward questions would she squeeze in today before I or Ava decided enough was enough and split? I prayed Ava wouldn't get too uncomfortable and leave. The beach had been my idea, and I didn't want it ruined for her. It had started off so well.

Miranda searched in her bag for something, chattering away about something she saw on television, and Ava leaned in and whispered to me, "I'm going to find a restroom. I think you should come too."

Beach restrooms were the filthiest, most insalubrious places on the planet, but anything beat sitting here with Miranda.

"Uh, Danielle, do you know where the restrooms are?" Ava asked.

"Over there. Wait, I'll show you. I need to go myself. Be back soon, Miranda. Are you all right watching Chester?"

She waved us away dismissively, thought nothing about our speedy departure.

We never made it to the restroom. Ava dragged me behind a wall, and we were alone at last. She snaked her tongue into my waiting mouth, and didn't come up for air until she'd stolen my breath from me.

"You have no idea how long I've wanted to do that," she

said.

I stood in her embrace, a sort of relief washing over me now that we could finally be affectionate. I sniffed her in, kissed and sucked at her neck. I was insatiable when it came to her. Nothing else mattered but holding her in my arms.

"This wasn't how I envisioned the day going," I said.

She let out a laugh. "I know. It's a tad messy, but I'm still having fun." She kissed my face; I closed my eyes and felt each kiss fall. I knew we didn't have much time, and that soon we would have to return to the group. I wanted to savor every kiss.

"Let's just leave. Right now. We can go for pizza or something. I just wanted it to be you, me and Chester."

"Hey, don't worry so much. Miranda's funny. I do feel sorry for her husband, though."

"You just can't help seeing the good in everyone, can you?" I said, sulking a little.

"Isn't that one of the reasons why you like me?"

We stayed there a few minutes more, but then someone walked past and we separated quickly, before returning to the others.

I couldn't kiss her goodbye that day, because Chester was there. But I did risk a brief stroke of her hand. That had become our replacement kiss when we were around others. We'd gotten good at doing it surreptitiously.

"Did you have fun today, honey?" I asked Chester when we were in the car and heading back home. I looked at him through the rear-view. Worn out and covered in sand.

He nodded tiredly.

"Were you happy that Emma came?"

"Yeah." He peered out the window, then turned back and looked at me. "I was happy that Miss Petal came too."

"So was I. You like her, don't you?"

He nodded. "Can she come with us the next time we go to the beach?"

"We'll see." If it were up to me she would accompany us everywhere. It embarrassed me slightly to admit to myself that I'd fallen so hard and so fast that I couldn't bear the thought of spending a moment away from her.

Dominic was waiting in the living room, finishing up a conversation (that didn't sound very child-friendly) when we got home.

"Hey, champ. How was the beach?" he asked when he'd hung up.

I dreaded what was coming next, knowing my son would never be able to keep his mouth shut about our day, and particularly who had been there with us.

As soon as Chester mentioned Miss Petal, Dominic shot me a look.

"Miss Petal was there, was she?"

"Yeah. And we played in the sea, and she taught me how to do a breaststroke."

"Did she also teach you how to do a breaststroke, Danielle?" he said.

He knew! There was no way he couldn't, not after that question.

I swallowed, tried not to panic. He couldn't prove anything. As far as anyone knew, Ava and I were just good friends. Nothing more. And jumping to the conclusion that we were lovers would have made anyone look delusional.

I glared at him. "What the hell are you talking about?"

"You didn't tell me she would be there."

"There was nothing to tell. I didn't know she would be there either."

"I find that hard to believe."

"Believe what you want, Dominic."

He followed me into the kitchen. "Why is it that she seems to go everywhere you go? Do you ever do anything alone any more?"

"She's a good friend, someone I like spending time with. But of course you would have a problem with that, wouldn't you? You don't like the thought of me having fun."

"Depends what kind of fun we're talking about."

He definitely knew! Oh, God. How long would it take for him to come out and say it?

"Just leave me alone," I said.

"Let me make something clear to you, Danielle." He towered over me, a menacing look in his eye. "If you try to make a fool of me, you'll be sorry." That was his last word before he stormed out of the room, leaving me feeling unsettled, shaken.

FOURTEEN

The dress, though tighter than it had been when I'd bought it six weeks prior, was a good choice. A backless navy blue number that hugged me in all the right places, gave my boobs a perkiness they hadn't had since my twenties. As I looked myself over in the full length mirror in the bathroom, I couldn't help but feel slightly smug.

The black heels weren't new, though I'd hardly worn them. They fit snugly. Peeking out behind my hair, which I'd worn down, my new diamond earrings sparkled.

I felt good as I checked out my ass. Wrapped up nicely, like a Christmas present, ready for my secret lover.

But as I left the bathroom that evening, Dominic's face appeared at the bottom of the stairs, reminding me that this wasn't going to be *that* sort of evening.

"Wow. Look at you. Who are you and what have you done with my wife?" He couldn't take his eyes off me, which only made me roll mine. He'd had me for eights years, and now he wanted to acknowledge me? What an ass!

"I'm still the same person. You know, the wife you keep reminding to shift the baby weight." At one time even thinking this would have made me bawl, but now his words had no effect. What he thought of me no longer mattered.

"I'd say you've shifted it well enough. Little Dominic is very impressed."

I made a face to show my disgust at his reference to his manhood. How had I ever found him attractive beyond the physical? Had I really been that shallow?

"Are we taking your car or mine?" I said.

"Mine, if you don't mind."

He was being nice to me. I didn't trust him when he was like this.

I sighed. "Fine." We locked up and got into his car. "I can't wait till this is over."

"I don't think Chester would be pleased to hear you say that. He's put a lot of effort into this performance."

I cut him a look. What the hell did he know? I was the one who'd helped Chester with the costume, the lines, the dance moves. I wasn't even sure Dominic knew what the play was about.

"It's not the play I have a problem with. It's having to keep up this charade with you in public. The sooner that's over, the better."

"Can't you try for just one evening to be civil?"

He was right. I needed to make the effort. If he could do it then I could too. Besides, it wasn't all bad. I would get to see Ava, and I hadn't seen her in two days. I'd already gotten withdrawal symptoms from her kisses, her body, her scent, her taste. I needed a new dose of the drug that I'd become addicted to.

I smiled to myself just thinking about her. The first thing I would do when I got to the school was take her somewhere quiet and play a much-needed game of tonsil tennis.

"When did you get the dress? It's nice." Dominic peered back and forth between me and the road ahead as he drove.

"A few weeks ago."

"Expensive?"

Why was he trying to make smalltalk? We were past all that. We weren't friends, just husband and wife.

"It was worth it," I said simply, looking at him skeptically. What was this about?

"You didn't wear it for me." It wasn't a question, more an observation, and an unusual one at that. What did it even mean?

"I wore it for myself."

"Yourself. Right." He nodded, didn't look at me, just carried on driving. And we didn't speak for the rest of the drive.

I was thankful to be out of the car, away from the thick tension in the air. And as soon as we locked up, we made our way into the school. I should have known something was off, that Dominic was up to something. Instead of walking ahead or behind me, as he usually did when we went out together, he stayed by my side. Even opened the doors for me.

In the cafeteria, refreshments were being served. We said our hellos to some of the other parents we knew. Entire families had come out for the big performance. The place was packed.

"You look a million and a half dollars!" Beth said when she saw me. She looked me up and down, impressed. "Really working that dress. Where have you been hiding that body?"

I'd managed to ditch Dominic a couple of minutes later, but before I knew it he was back by my side. He put an arm around my waist.

"She looks great, doesn't she?" he concurred, and kissed me on the cheek with affection. More affection than he'd shown me in years.

Unfortunately, his timing was dreadful. It just so happened that as the kiss landed, Ava walked into the cafeteria. She spotted me immediately. The smile she'd been wearing slipped from her face.

"I'm going to have a hard time keeping my eyes, and hands, off her," he added, and wasn't quiet about it.

"Cut it out, Dominic," I said, trying to wriggle free without making it too obvious that his touch repulsed me. All our friends were in the room but so too was Ava. This wasn't a display I wanted her to see.

"What's wrong with you?" Beth gawked at me, flabbergasted. "Your husband can't keep his hands off you and all you have to say is cut it out. Some people don't deserve nice things."

Ava didn't come over, but instead greeted some of the other parents. All the while Dominic stuck on to me, as though glued to my side. He wouldn't let go.

"Shall we go say hello to Miss Petal?" he asked jovially.

"No," I said quickly. "I'll speak to her later maybe."

But it became apparent moments later that I had no choice in the matter. He practically dragged me over to her, his arm placed firmly around my waist. Why was he doing this to me?

"Good evening," he said to her.

She forced a smile, which didn't reach her eyes. I knew her well enough to know when she was faking it.

"Hi Mr. Thomas. Hi Danielle." She peered down at the hand gripping my waist, then back up at me. The look in her eye crushed me.

"We're really looking forward to the performance," Dominic said. "Proud parents, you know how it is. Even if he had one line, we'd be here cheering him on."

She smiled again, and I tried my hardest to pull away from Dominic without it looking suspicious, but it was no use.

"Oh, before I forget. I wanted to thank you for helping my wife pick this dress. I assume it was you, at least. Well, good job. Doesn't she look fantastic?"

"Actually, I had nothing to do with it. But yes, she does."

Dominic leaned forward and whispered, "Between you and me, I'm having a hard time simply looking and not touching. I think an early night will be in order tonight." He winked, and I felt his hand slip onto my butt.

Ava didn't even try to fake a smile this time. It was likely impossible. She'd seen the hand move too.

That was where I drew the line. I shoved his hand off. "Enough," I said through gritted teeth.

"Would you both excuse me?" She didn't wait for an answer, just hastened out of the room. I tried to go after her, but Dominic's grip on me was tighter than ever.

"You stay here, beside your husband." It was an order, and he didn't even look at me when he said it.

"What the hell was that?" I muttered, furiously.

He didn't respond, just led me away to talk to some more of our friends.

I didn't get to speak to her again before the show started, which meant I couldn't enjoy any of it. She was working behind the scenes, getting the children into their costumes, helping them with their lines and stage positions. I hated the thought that while she worked she had the image of Dominic's filthy hands all over me.

I sneaked away minutes before the end of the show, before Dominic could stop me or tag along uninvited. I needed to see her, to straighten everything out. I sent her a text to say I would be waiting in the parking lot. A part of me thought she wouldn't come, that she was so furious with me that she would leave me waiting there forever.

When I saw the doors open and everyone pour out, I knew she wasn't coming, and that I would have to find her myself.

"Mom, what did you think of the play?" Chester came running out to greet me, Dominic not far behind him. The latter gave me a look I couldn't decipher. It was as if he knew I was waiting for Ava.

I embraced my son, squeezing him tightly. "It was terrific. You were awesome, honey. I'm so proud of you."

"I didn't forget my lines," he said gleefully. It had been a real concern for him that he would.

"I told you you had this in the bag." I ruffled his hair. "My little superstar. How about ice cream, huh? Beth said she's taking Jack too. We could tag along." Posing it as a question was pointless; what seven-year-old would turn down ice cream?

He climbed into the car, and I waited until Dominic had gotten in before announcing that I needed to use the ladies' room. Dominic cut me a scathing look, and I knew then that the whole charade earlier had been for Ava's benefit. He'd wanted her to see us like that, as a married couple; he'd wanted to hurt her. Which meant only one thing: he knew about us. I'd suspected for a while that this was the case, hearing his snide, ambiguous comments whenever he brought her up.

"Don't forget to wash your hands," he called after me, and I heard the bitterness in his voice.

Ava was in the middle of a conversation with another teacher when I knocked on her classroom door. Normally I wouldn't have disturbed them, knowing that I would get to see her later, at her place, uninterrupted. But this couldn't wait.

"Hi Miss Petal. Sorry to bother you. Do you have a minute?"

"I'm actually in the middle of something–" she started, but the other teacher cut in, said she would talk to her later, and left us alone.

"Why won't you look at me?" I said. Her head was still down.

"Honestly, Dani? Because I can't."

My heart shattered into a thousand pieces to hear her say that. Once she'd told me that she could look at me all day long and never have the desire to do anything else. Now this.

"I'm sorry. I'm so sorry." I rushed to her, took her hand, but it was limp in mine. She didn't want me to touch her. "I never wanted you to ever see that. It's Dominic, he's playing games. He wants everyone to think we're happy." I didn't tell her that he more than likely knew about us, and that his actions had been out of spite.

"And you made it easy for him. It was so easy for him to put his hands on you, like you were a prize. And you did nothing to stop him."

"What could I do? He's my husband."

She finally looked at me, and her eyes were a mixture of melancholy and ire. She'd never looked at me like that before. So cold, yet so hurt. I just wanted to hold her in my arms and make everything go away.

"And what am I to you?"

"You're...you're my lover." I shrugged hopelessly. What was I supposed to say? "You're my best friend. What he did doesn't change any of that."

The breath she let out was rattly, shaky. "It changes everything, Danielle. He had every right to do that to you, because he's your husband...and I'm just your lover."

"It isn't like that at all." I was losing the battle and growing frantic. I just didn't seem to have the right words. "Please don't do this, Ava. I–"

"I really can't see you right now. I'm sorry. I just...I can't talk to you. It hurts too much." Her voice cracked, and she turned away quickly so that I couldn't see her cry.

"Ava..."

"Please, I just need some time, all right?"

FIFTEEN

Leaving her that evening was the hardest thing I'd ever had to do. But without the right words, without knowing what they were, I couldn't make it better. It was exactly as we'd both said, and only now had we truly realized what the implications of that were: I was somebody else's wife.

I didn't say a word to Dominic when I climbed into the car. And I barely spoke a word at the ice cream parlor. I wanted to go straight home, but since I'd already promised Chester the treat, I had to sit through it, miserably.

It was after nine when Chester finally went down. I'd managed to keep my cool for more than two hours. An achievement, considering I was boiling up inside.

But as soon as my son was fast asleep, worn out from the long day, a dam inside me burst.

The sound of the television playing in the living room told me where Dominic was. I found him lounging on the couch watching highlights from a game, a beer clutched in his hand. I snatched up the remote and switched off the TV.

"What are you doing, Danielle? Turn it back on."

The devil was in me when I hurled the remote across the room. It smashed against the wall. It would have to be replaced at some point, but in my rage, none of that mattered.

"What the hell is wrong with you?" he demanded, shooting up from the couch.

"How dare you!" I pointed a shaky finger at him, my blood having reached boiling point.

"What?"

"You don't get to do that. You don't ever get to touch me again, you piece of crap." My hair shook wildly when I screamed at him.

He sneered back at me. "Did I upset someone, huh?" He wasn't referring to me.

"That's the last time I ever let you come near me, do you hear me? The last time. Even if I have to break your hand to get you off. I don't care who's watching."

"You keep forgetting something, Dani. I own you. Sickness and health, death do us part, remember?"

"Bullshit! And you can take this too." I wrested off my wedding ring. It had been off many times while I was with Ava – while I was inside her. Removing it for good would save me time later.

I tossed it at him. "Those words, our vows, this ring, everything about us is a farce. And I'm done playing the doting wife in public. That stunt you pulled this evening, that was the last of it."

I said these words more for my own benefit than his. As a promise to myself that no matter what the circumstance, I would never again pretend to be happy with him.

"You foolish little bitch!" he hissed. "You think you've got it all figured out, don't you? You get a smidgeon of attention and now you think you're a new woman." He grabbed me by the arm, and I couldn't break free. He was so strong, so angry. "Well I've got news for you, princess. Life can get pretty fucking uncomfortable out there for you if you want to go down this route. You want to make a fool of me?" he screamed, spit hitting my face. "I'll destroy you, Danielle. Don't fuck with me!"

He shoved me away. These were sides of each other we had never shown, and his side terrified me.

But that wasn't going to stop me. I scowled at him one final time before storming off. In the hallway I pulled on my jacket, grabbed my car keys. He watched me from the living room door.

"Just remember what I said. You go down this route, you're finished. You and the little whore you're running off to."

I said nothing, just slammed out of that house as fast as I could. As I drove, my eyes blurry with tears, my head cloudy with all the thoughts colliding, I wondered how long he'd known about us. At which point had my infidelity become apparent? He'd been dropping hints, making ambiguous comments for weeks, but had never expressly said it until now.

I trembled as I drove, unable to drive straight. It was a relief to make it to Ava's house in one piece.

It took me a couple of minutes, sitting behind the wheel, parked outside her house, to work up the courage to step out.

I hammered on the door when my ringing went unanswered. Wasn't she home yet? And if not, where was she? With whom?

But then I heard the faint sound of footsteps descending the stairs. The hallway light flicked on. Seconds later the door opened. A sheer, frilly nightgown clad Ava stared back at me, her brow furrowed in confusion.

"Dani, what are you–"

"Please, I know you said you needed time, and that you didn't want to see me, but this can't wait."

She let me in, and I followed her into the living room. Now I stood before her, feeling slightly hopeless. All I wanted was to take her in my arms, hold her, feel the warmth of her body against mine. The simple things in life.

There was still hurt in her eyes.

"Look, I need you to know something," I started. "Just hear me out."

"Okay."

"I never wanted him to touch me, and he is never going to do that again. I am so sorry I let him, and I'm sorry you had to see that."

Her breathing was heavy, labored. She said nothing.

"I messed up. Not just with that, but with you, after. I didn't have the words to express it then, but I do now. You asked me what you were to me." Tears filled my eyes but didn't fall immediately. I sniffed, stepped closer to her. "Everything. That's what you are to me. He's my husband, but you're my everything."

Her face softened, but she still remained silent.

"You have my heart, Ava."

"But he has your body..."

I shook my head vehemently, put my hands on her waist. "No, you have that too. I'm yours, and only yours. Heart, body and soul. Now please make love to me the way only you can."

She smashed her lips to mine. She couldn't exercise patience in stripping me bare any more than I could her. My clothes were torn from my body and carelessly tossed everywhere.

She took me on the soft rug – we didn't even make it to the couch. She laid me on my back, pinned my arms above my head, made me look at her, see her.

"You *are* mine," she said. "Mind, body and soul." A repeat of my own words for affirmation.

I nodded, and she kissed me again, rougher than usual. And when she slotted her naked body between my legs and I felt her wetness combine with my own, I knew that our love-making would be just as rough.

Her grinding was powerful, slow but with lots of pressure. We held each other's gaze while she raked her sex against mine. My body jerked beneath her, like a rag doll's. The happiest rag doll on Earth.

She kept me pinned down the whole time, our bodies pressed together. It was a glorious feeling to be so connected to her. We became one that night like we never had before.

And we came within seconds of each other, as close to simultaneous as we'd ever come.

She took my face in one hand, held me by my chin, and her eyes were filled with love. "You're everything to me too," she said. She'd presumably fucked all her aggression away, because now her touch and kiss were nothing but tender.

Twenty minutes later and we hadn't moved from the floor. Only now, she'd pulled the couch throw down to act as a blanket.

I lay on my stomach on the plush rug, barely covered up by the makeshift blanket, while she laid slow, wet kisses on my back and butt. I giggled every now and then when they tickled.

"Aren't you tired of kissing me there by now?" I said. While any kind of kiss from her, no matter its location, was appreciated, I wanted her lips on mine more than anything.

"Nope," she said between kisses. "I'll never get tired of kissing you."

I laughed and let her carry on. Eventually she kissed a trail up my back, along the back of my neck. She settled on top of me, pressing her naked weight against my flesh. I felt everything: the erect nipples, the moistness between her thighs as it clung to my buttocks. Soon I would be aroused all over again, if she wasn't careful.

"Say it again," she whispered, whilst kissing the side of my face.

I knew exactly what it was. "I love you."

She turned me over, kissed me. "And again."

"I love you." I was laughing now. I'd said it half a dozen times already that night.

She brushed her lips across mine. "And I love you, Danielle. I mean, I don't roll around on the floor naked with any old person."

We laughed lazily, tiredly.

"This is the first time I've done it on the floor," I said. "How very common of us. And I love it! Who needs a bed, right?"

We kissed and kissed for several more minutes, on the verge of another round of beautiful love-making, but we cuddled instead.

"I had a dream about you last night," she said.

"What was I doing in the dream? Something naughty?"

"Actually, it was a dream about you and Chester. I dreamed that you moved in with me."

I was quiet for a moment, because it was so unexpected. And timely.

Then I snuggled closer in her arms. "That sounds like a wonderful dream."

It was her turn to fall silent. I sensed that she was weighing up whether or not to say what she had planned. And then she did. "Can it ever be a reality?"

"If it were just me I had to look out for, I would move in with you tomorrow. But with Chester, it's not that simple."

"I know. I know. I don't want to pressure you. I just... It was a dream I didn't want to wake from, that's all."

She was so honest, always. About everything. And I had been too, mostly. But I stayed quiet over the fight I'd had prior to seeing her. About the conversation with Dominic. About his threats. I didn't tell her that he knew. I had my reasons, the most pertinent being that, as much as I loved her and wanted to be with her, I wasn't ready to *be* with her. It wasn't just about starting a new relationship. My life was so particular, and being Dominic's wife was heavily ingrained in that. There was also the little business of her being female, and my son's teacher.

In other words, it was a messy affair. If she'd known that I'd virtually come out to my husband, that he knew I was in love with her, I was sure she would push me to take those big steps. Steps I was ill-prepared to take.

So I kept shtum and let her lavish her love on me. I felt a bit like a leech – taking, and giving nothing in return.

SIXTEEN

In my mind I'd left Dominic over a year ago, months before Ava's arrival. We'd been sleeping in separate beds for nearly two years, after he'd given me an STI. Continuing to live in the same house was more out of convenience than any hope of working things out down the road and getting back together. At least, that was how I saw it. The cheating was one thing, but the STI, that changed everything. Sadness transformed into bitterness that had eventually – where we now sat – morphed into hatred. He'd never had a shot at winning me back, I just hadn't told him that.

Perhaps I should have. Not that he'd made any attempt to win my heart again. He'd always pictured us growing old together, while he banged every woman within a one hundred mile radius! His parents had been married fifty years, and they adored me. It made sense to keep the farce going. Disappointing them, and then reaching seventy and realizing you were completely alone thanks to losing the one woman crazy enough to marry you, wasn't in his plans.

He'd never banked on me finding someone else. He'd spent years making me feel unattractive, hinting that no one else would want me. All part of his scheme to keep me loyal, keep me by his side.

And now, I was searching for a small two-bed house close to Ava's place. Something temporary while I sorted my life out. Business was going fine, and I could afford to leave.

I sat in the dining room, my web browser open on one of the local real estate websites. I'd spent all morning searching, finding the whole thing terrifying but at the same time exciting. New beginnings were always scary.

"Naive," Dominic whispered by my ear, prompting me to jump and spill some of my coffee on the table. I'd been so engrossed in reading property descriptions, that I hadn't heard him come in. He'd been out all morning.

"What are you talking about?" I got a napkin and wiped up the spillage.

"You, trying to move out. I think it's naive."

I didn't like his smirk. It was only slightly less troubling than the side of him I'd seen a couple of weeks prior, on the night of our big bust up.

"Your opinion is of no concern to me." I returned to the screen and continued reading. A garden, a garage with space for one car. No pets.

He laughed. "Who's the second room for?"

"Don't ask stupid questions."

"It can't possibly be for Chester, because he isn't going anywhere."

He was trying to get my back up, and I wasn't going to let him. He couldn't stop me from leaving with my son. My rights as a mother would forever trump his. I had always been the more involved parent. He wouldn't stand a chance up against me in court, if it ever came to that.

"We'll see, Dominic," I said levelly. No use arguing. I was more than confident of my position.

"We shall," he said smugly. "Isn't it funny how little we think things through sometimes? We make these rash decisions without knowing what life has in store for us. Without realizing that it could all come crashing down in the blink of an eye."

What was he talking about now? Oh, what did it matter? I tutted, picked up my laptop and left the room. I wasn't going to give him an audience.

As soon as Ava opened the door that evening, I knew something was wrong. Her eyes were missing some of the spark I'd grown accustomed to.

"Would you like a drink?" she offered.

"No, I want you to tell me what's wrong."

"I don't want to talk about it right now. Can you kiss me first?"

I kissed her, and kissed her again, because it looked like she needed it more than air.

We sat down with a glass of red wine, which I barely touched. We talked around her problem, and I grew more and more impatient. It was obvious she had something on her mind.

Then, unable to take it anymore, I took her glass out of her hand and set it down. I kept hold of her hand. "What is it?"

"Nothing really. It's my problem. I can handle it."

"Your problems are mine now, or had you forgotten that I'm a part of your life?"

"No, I definitely didn't forget..." She looked away miserably.

"Okay, what's going on?"

"Have Mrs. Hawthorne or Mrs. Ross said anything to you about our friendship being...inappropriate?"

I frowned. "Miranda and Beth? No. What sort of question is that?" I was growing more confused by the second.

"The principal called me in for a meeting after school today. Apparently a couple of parents have made a complaint about you and me spending time together. Said that it was unprofessional because it sent the wrong message and encouraged favoritism."

"What?" I exclaimed, outraged. "That's nonsense! What right does anyone have to complain because two grown women are friends?"

"They think Chester will get special treatment over the other children."

"My God! Those bastards! I can't believe this." I was more appalled than she was, it seemed. Maybe she'd already been through this when she first heard the news. "Did he say who the parents were? And he actually said parents, as in more than one?"

"He said the identities were confidential."

I shook my head in disbelief. "I just can't imagine Beth or Miranda or anyone else I know doing something like this. Or caring enough about it. Not to mention the fact that all the parents love you, love what you've done for their children. I don't get this."

She shrugged tiredly. "Neither do I. But that's what he said. While he can't stop me spending time with you, he does think our talks in school should from now on be brief and only about Chester."

"That's bullshit!" It wasn't unreasonable to expect that our conversations in school only pertain to school business, but the fact that this man was, in essence, compelling her to stop being my friend in public, rankled me. "Where the hell does he get off, huh?"

"It's okay, Dani, honest." She kissed my face to calm me down, and it worked for a minute. "I see you almost every evening anyway. He can't take that away from us."

"But–"

She pressed a finger to my lips to silence me, before replacing her finger with her lips. If anything could placate me, it was her kiss. "Let's not let this ruin our evening."

"Okay. I'll try."

I remained in a weird mood for the rest of the night, racking my brains trying to figure out what asshole had run squealing to the principal. Beth and Miranda had both used the term "special treatment", but in jest. I didn't want to believe that they were behind this.

We watched some stand-up comedy on television, her way of lightening the mood, and then we cuddled. Time seemed to speed by when we were together, and before long it was time for me to go. It was a school night, and I needed to get back to Chester. We'd settled on one as the cut off time, though we frequently ran over.

"Ugh, I hate this part," I grumbled, not wanting to get up. My limbs felt heavy. Heavy with reluctance.

"There is a way you can avoid this part entirely..."

"That's not an option right now, Ava, you know that." She was, of course, referring to me moving in with her. Ever since the dream, she'd brought it up every time we met. And where another person might have grown annoyed after hearing it six times, it only reminded me that there was someone who loved me enough to want me around all the time. It reminded me of her love for me.

"I have to ask in case one day you say yes." She kissed my cheek. Never disheartened by my rejection of the idea, just happy to be with me.

I almost told her about the house hunting, but decided against it. It was still early days. I didn't want to bring it up until I'd at least been to some viewings.

It was impossible to look at the other parents and not see traitors among me. In the playground, in the grocery store, passing by in the street. They would all smile and greet me, as always. But then I would wonder, wonder what lay beneath each friendly gesture. These people I'd known for years, some of them very well, some as friends. I didn't know who to trust.

It went on like that for two weeks, me looking at everyone as a possible suspect. Especially when Ava and I shared brief words in front of them. Who was watching? Who had a problem with it?

That was no way to live. If someone was out to get me, I sure as hell wasn't just going to sit back and play nice. I wanted to at least rule out the people I considered friends.

"Please don't mention it to anyone, Dani," Ava had pleaded the night she told me. "Just let it go."

I'd agreed to do as she asked, but after two weeks the not knowing was driving me crazy.

It was a Thursday, and Miranda and I were sitting on one of the school benches in the playground, waiting for the 3:30 bell.

"...So now she's wild about horses. Says she wants one for her ninth birthday." She rolled her eyes dramatically. "Kids just have no idea how much things cost. Although, given her track record with keeping pets alive, it wouldn't be an expense we'd have for long!" She gave her usual, soulful laugh, always much louder than the joke required.

Beth arrived and joined us. Now was my chance.

"Guys, I wanted to ask you something. About my friendship with Miss Petal."

They looked at me, frowning and clueless. It could have all been an act, though.

"What about it?" Beth asked.

"I know you've both hinted that you thought Chester would get special treatment, due to our friendship..."

Miranda laughed. "Come on, Dani, you know we were just fooling around."

"Yeah, what is this?"

"Well, someone has a problem with it. Someone complained to the principal. Thinks it's inappropriate, and that it's unfair to the other kids."

They both wore the same expression: one of outrage.

It wasn't them. Whatever else these women were, they hadn't stabbed me in the back. I should have listened to my gut on this one.

"And you thought it was one of us? Gee, Dani, do you really think that low of us? But worst of all, do you really think we have nothing better to do?" Miranda laughed, but I could see in her eyes that I'd offended her.

"No," I said. "I'm sorry I even asked. Of course it wasn't you. But it was someone. Maybe you've heard something? A whisper from one of the other parents?"

Beth shook her head. "That's not the type of thing people around here do, or even think, for that matter. You must have an enemy. You or Miss Petal. But why the principal would pay any attention to a complaint like that is anybody's guess."

It came as no small relief to learn that my friends weren't traitors. I just hoped our friendship hadn't been damaged by my accusations, however subtle they'd been.

But after a couple of minutes it was business as usual, and Miranda went on babbling. Though the mystery remained unsolved, at least I'd ruled them out.

"Next week is the big 4-0, as you well know," Miranda went on.

"Of course. You haven't stopped talking about it for months," I said.

"Only because I don't want anyone telling me they've forgotten, and no one turns up on the day. I've gone to a lot of expense for this party."

"We'll all be there, Miranda," Beth said impatiently.

"Wouldn't miss it for the world."

She turned to me. "And what about you, missy? You won't let me down, will you?"

"Of course not."

"You're welcome to bring Miss Petal if you like. She's a lot of fun. And it'll be a big screw you to anyone who has a problem with your friendship."

"So I can bring her instead of Dominic?" I asked hopefully.

She frowned. "Why would you do that? Bring them both. Fred already told Dominic about it anyway."

I shifted uneasily in my seat. There was no way Dominic and Ava at the same party would be a good thing. One I wanted to come. The other had every right to come. I just prayed Dominic would be too busy to make it. I had to start getting people used to seeing me and Ava out together. This would be the perfect opportunity.

SEVENTEEN

"We're going to be late if you don't cut that out," Ava giggled. My face was buried in her neck, my arms wrapped around her chest, my hands fondling her breasts. Peeled down around her waist was her dress, whose zip I'd been tasked with doing up...

"I don't care. They won't miss us." I kissed and kissed her neck, and let my hands pull one of her breasts from the bra. Her laughter trailed off and became heavy breathing as she let me caress her teat. The glorious moment came as the nipple hardened in my hand.

"Mmm, I never get tired of feeling that," I said.

I had no access barred reign of her body, and I wasn't holding back. I was like a cat in heat – no, *ten* cats in heat – whenever I was alone with her.

"You're bad for me," she breathed. "That's the last time I ask you to help me with my dress."

"I did help you with your dress... I helped you take it down."

She laughed, and I continued to fondle her. We were in her bedroom, the bed was a mere few feet away. But we had a party to get to, and I already knew how much Miranda hated lateness.

"Is this your way of getting as much of me as you can because we won't be able to touch while we're there?"

"Something like that." I twisted her around to face me so I could kiss her properly. Her lips were now mine. Everything was mine, and I was a proud owner. "But mostly I just can't keep my hands off you. It's an affliction I'll never get over."

We kissed some more, touched even more than that, but she had to call time, otherwise we never would have left the house.

An hour later, we were on our first drink at Miranda's house. It was a big turn out – close to two hundred people. Most I didn't know, but some were parents from the school. Couples far outnumbered singles. It seemed most women had come with their husbands, and certainly not their "gal pals".

It had worked out well for me that Dominic said he had a prior engagement (read: some blonde he wanted to screw) and thus couldn't make it. Only when I'd gotten confirmation that he wasn't coming did I invite Ava.

We were standing in the garden, wine glasses in hand, talking to two other couples we knew from Chester's school.

"It's great to see you here, Miss Petal. I'm glad you came," Miranda said as she passed briefly.

"Thanks for inviting me."

She fit right in with everyone. They loved her, and these two couples, despite their promise not to talk shop, had been singing her praises since we arrived. So and so loved her, wouldn't stop talking about her. Had learned so much. And on and on. No one wanted to speak to me, no siree.

But I had never been happier. Standing by and watching everyone fawn over my girlfriend reassured me that, when the time came, they would all welcome her with open arms as my partner. Maybe I was naive in thinking that, but it kept the smile glued to my face.

"See, I told you you would do fine," I said when we were alone, having excused ourselves. She'd been worried that people wouldn't treat her as one of them, just as the woman who taught their children.

"I'm actually having a lot of fun."

"Me too." I leaned in a little closer, though not enough to look too suspicious, like two women in love. "But I would be even happier if I could kiss those beautiful lips of yours right now, in front of all these people."

"Well, you could do that, but you'd have a lot of explaining to do," she laughed.

It would have been the perfect setting to showcase my newfound love. But at the same time doing so would have exposed me as a cheat. No matter how many extramarital affairs Dominic had under his belt that I knew about, these people were still oblivious. He managed to play the faithful, doting husband so well in front of them. Only with me did the mask fall.

We were still laughing to ourselves when my eyes fell on the glass door leading out to the garden. My laughter cut out abruptly, so much so that it caused Ava to stop too.

"What is it?" she asked.

"Dominic's here," I said. I felt the blood rushing to my head, felt my heart pounding wildly. A sense of doom washed over me.

"I thought you said he couldn't make it."

"That's what he said." The lying sack of shit! As his gaze met mine, the smirk that spread across his face told me this had been his plan all along. Turning up when he knew Ava would be here with me.

"But that's not a problem, is it?"

Of course it's a problem, my inner voice screamed. But she didn't know. I still hadn't told her that he knew about us, that when he looked at her now he saw the woman who was screwing his wife, his property. And that he wasn't taking any of it well. So how would she have known that his being here was nothing but revenge?

"I think we should go," I mumbled.

But Dominic had made his way over to us, beer in hand, shit-eating grin taking up half his face.

"Miss Petal, what a pleasure to see you again," he said jovially. Too bad it was all an act, and seemingly one only I could see through.

"You too, Mr. Thomas."

"Oh, we don't need to be formal. It's Dominic. You and my wife are so close now, you're almost family. It's as though there are three people in this marriage."

The unease in her laugh was obvious.

"What are you doing here, Dominic?" I asked, trying to keep my voice level.

"I was invited, wasn't I, honey? It almost sounds like you don't want me here."

I said nothing. And a few moments later, Beth and her husband joined us. I wanted to make a quick escape, but before long Ava was pulled into a conversation by Beth's husband. The Blakes, Miranda's neighbors, joined us, joined in the conversation. Dominic and I, however, were the only ones not speaking. Instead I was scowling at him while he smirked back.

There always comes a time when you know the shit's about to hit the fan. The air gets heavy, the sky becomes overcast. Your stomach rumbles as if warning you to expect the worst. I wondered how long it would take before Dominic did what he'd come here to do.

He lasted half an hour.

"There's this town in Brazil I read about where there are virtually no men. Most of the women are really attractive and are desperate for more men to move into the area, lest they die unmarried," Beth's husband said eagerly. A man who was usually very quiet had come out of his shell by talking travel with Ava.

Beth laughed. "So that's why you wanted to go to Brazil this summer. You were looking for a replacement!" she teased.

He chuckled. "You know you're the only woman who would ever put up with me, Beth." He kissed her on the cheek.

"That sounds like the sort of place you would thrive in, Ava," Dominic said casually, taking a sip of his beer.

She looked at him blankly. "How so?"

"Well, nice weather, nice people, no men around..."

"That sounds like the ideal place for me, too!" Beth said.

"Yeah, but after a while it would get a little boring, don't you think? You know, not having men around?" This came from Mrs. Blake. "I know I couldn't do it. What happens when they need to...you know? Does Ann Summers ship to that part of the world?" She laughed at her own joke.

"You don't think they use each other, do you?" Dominic asked, his shock fake and exaggerated. "I mean, does that sort of thing really happen outside of pornography? A town full of women, no men around, so they decide to take care of each other? What do you think, Ava?"

I saw her face, the way her smile had disappeared. Her breathing was unsteady, her cheeks rosy. She knew what was happening, and she had no way of stopping it.

"I don't know. I try not to comment on what other people do in their bedrooms."

"No, I don't believe they would sleep with each other." Mrs. Blake shuddered, made a face as though the thought disgusted her. Ava saw it, looked away. "Straight women, who have only ever been attracted to men, would never." The ignorance was astounding. I wanted to scream at this dinosaur, remind her that she was living in the twenty-first century.

"You would think that. I mean, going from wanting one organ to settling for another, as though they're interchangeable. It doesn't sit right," Dominic said, shaking his head, looking at me.

The painfully ignorant Mrs. Blake moaned in agreement. "I have gay friends, so I don't mean any offense by this, but I'll never understand that sort of thing."

I'm sure my face matched Ava's upon hearing that. Intolerance and homophobia, so easily shared, as if they were discussing a new movie or something. I wanted to leave, to walk away from this woman. I should have grabbed Ava's hand and marched my girlfriend away, because there was only one direction in which this night could go now, and it wasn't up.

"Hey, just because these women live in a village without men, doesn't mean they don't travel elsewhere to meet some," Beth's husband jumped in.

Dominic shrugged. "But I'm sure many just settle, find the effort of searching too troublesome. What would you do in that situation, Ava?"

"I don't know," she mumbled, eyes down on the drink in her hand.

"Oh, I forgot. You would be more than happy in that situation. Why do I keep forgetting?" Dominic added.

Beth's brow furrowed. "What does that mean?"

"Dominic," I warned in a stern voice.

He laughed. "What? We're all adults. I think it's healthy to talk about these things. Miss Petal might be a teacher, but she's still an adult. And good on the principal for being so progressive. I've heard out-LGBT teachers have a much harder time getting jobs than their straight counterparts."

Now all eyes, bar mine, were on Ava. I couldn't look at her, not without it breaking my heart.

"I don't follow," Beth's husband said, his brow furrowed deeply. "Does that mean–"

"That I'm gay? Yes, that's exactly what it means." Ava swallowed down the rest of her wine. "Now if you'd excuse me, I'm going to head home. Nice to see all of you."

She hastened away before I could stop her. But...I never had any intention of stopping her, or going after her. We'd arrived together, by cab, and now we were leaving separately.

"Well, that was quite unexpected," Beth said, looking around the circle, dumbfounded. "I never would have guessed. I expect all gay women to look like Ellen DeGeneres!"

"I always did get that vibe from her when I spoke to her," Mr. Blake said, turning up his nose as though he smelled something rotten. "She never seemed interested in any of the men, and you'd think at least one of us would have caught her eye."

"They come in all shapes and sizes, Beth. Some of them might even look like you, or maybe my wife over there..."

The look I shot Dominic could have scorched his skin, it was that fiery. But the more I glowered, the more he smiled.

I tossed and turned all night, kicking the covers off in frustration, throwing the pillows across the room when I couldn't get them right. I didn't get much sleep, and whenever I started dozing off, the image of Ava's face, deflated and dejected, sprung back into my mind.

I couldn't sleep because I knew I'd messed up. I should have gone after her, like any loving partner would. But doing so would have been too telling.

If you really loved her, nothing would have stopped you.

If you really loved her, what they thought wouldn't matter.
If you really loved her, you would be with her right now.

I did love her, I had the heartache to prove it, but I was weak. A coward of the highest order. I'd seen the ignorance, the intolerance, witnessed it as an onlooker, comfortable from my seat out of the line of fire, and I knew I couldn't hack it. They didn't understand her, so they sure as hell wouldn't understand me.

I waited until the following evening, Sunday, to see her. I'd put it off for twenty-four hours and couldn't any longer. It wasn't that I didn't want to see her, but that I felt awful, somehow responsible for what happened at the party.

When she opened the door, she did so with little enthusiasm, as though reluctant. I thought that when she saw it was me her mood would change.

"Hi," I said, stepping inside.

"Hi." Her voice sounded tired, lethargic. She looked it, too.

I followed her into the living room. She didn't offer me any of the wine she was drinking, despite the bottle being half full.

She sat down with her glass, drank from it and said nothing, just watched me, waiting for me to speak.

"About the other night..." I wrung my hands, feeling lost for the first time in front of her, and in her house. I didn't feel welcome.

"What about the other night?" She wasn't going to make this easy for me.

"I had no idea Dominic was going to say all of that. I'm sorry."

"How long has he known about us? He does know, doesn't he? Otherwise he wouldn't have put on that display."

I nodded solemnly. "I didn't tell him, he figured it out."

"How long?" she demanded.

"I'm not sure. He's been dropping hints for a while, but I

don't know exactly."

"And that display at the play? That was for my benefit?"

I nodded.

"Why didn't you tell me?"

I shrugged helplessly. "I didn't want to worry you. I should have, I know, but I just... Look, I hate how this has happened. And I'm sorry you had to go through all of that yesterday, being outed like that."

"I don't care that they know, Danielle. I'm not ashamed of who I am." She said this in a tone that sounded very accusatory. And the scathing look that accompanied it, that she shot at me, gave me goosebumps.

I hurried to sit beside her, rested my hand on her thigh. "I'll never forgive myself for not going after you."

"You would do the exact same thing if you had a do-over, let's be honest." I thought she would push my hand away, but she let it sit there. She was mad, furious, but not enough that my touch no longer meant anything to her. "You stayed with your husband and your friends. You were right where you were supposed to be."

"That's not true. Where I'm supposed to be is with you. We were happy until he showed up. That was real."

She didn't look convinced. "That was an illusion." My hand fell off her leg when she got up. I got the feeling she did it purposefully. She walked to the window, her thinking spot.

"What is that supposed to mean?" I questioned.

"Nothing. Just that the future we envisioned for ourselves, or rather the future I envisioned for us, won't be possible."

"Are you giving up on me?"

She stared at me. Before we started our affair, there hadn't been a moment when I hadn't seen her smiling. Since I'd arrived that evening, she had yet to crack a smile. Could I really have been causing more misery than joy? The thought terrified me.

"No." She sighed, and her shoulders sagged. "I'm just disillusioned, that's all."

I went to her, even though she didn't ask me to. I stood before her, helpless, so she could see that I was just as hurt as she was. But most of all, I needed her arms around me. It was selfish of me expecting it when she was the one who'd been embarrassed the night before. But her hugs, her kisses, were like my lifeblood on a bad day.

"I love you. If you remember nothing else, remember that," I said. Her mouth was closed, her arms folded, but I kissed her anyway, let my lips linger. And eventually she opened her mouth and gave in, allowing our tongues to do their familiar dance. And soon her arms were around me, where they belonged.

I was still in her bad books, so once our lips parted ways, I said, "I've been house-hunting for a couple of weeks."

The first sign of a smile. "Really?"

"Really. I have a couple of viewings lined up this week."

"That is the best news I've heard all day. Why didn't you open with that?"

"Because I needed to apologize first. Grovel. Plead. Beg..." I kissed her, and she squeezed me tighter.

"Where have you been looking?"

"Not too far from the school. And you..."

Now the smile was back in full force. "Well, that's a good compromise if I can't have you here."

We made love that night, and although it was beautiful, I felt the storm cloud hanging over us. The elephant in the room that neither of us wanted to talk about. That what happened at the party wasn't something we could ignore, hide away from, if we ever wanted a future outside of the bedroom. And that, despite my words now, the fact remained that I'd let her leave the party, without going after her, without supporting her.

As I fell asleep in her arms, I prayed that I never had to make that decision again, even though I knew it was inevitable. Because I still wasn't sure if I could do what was required of me...

And then the ultimate test came the following week.

EIGHTEEN

I shook the real estate agent's hand. She was a young woman, all business, and very good at what she did. Unfortunately, she couldn't spin her magic with the three properties she showed me that day. One too small, one far too big, and the other...well, it was perfect...until the neighbor came out and informed me that the previous owner had abducted and killed two women in the house. No thanks. I'd had enough bad luck as it was.

"I'll give you a call when we have something else for you. We have a couple coming on the market that I'm sure you'll love."

I thanked her and went on my way. Now that I was truly serious about moving, nothing seemed right. It wasn't that I didn't want to – on the contrary, Dominic had turned up the obnoxious dial big time, and I couldn't bear being in the house with him. The new house needed to be the right fit, not just for me but for Chester. And the move, as seamless as possible.

I glanced at the dashboard clock. Perfect timing. I had fifteen minutes to get to school to do the pick up.

I sung along to some of the seventies songs that came on the radio, feeling more cheerful than I had in the past week. I hadn't seen much of Ava, as she'd started an evening Mandarin class three times a week, in preparation for a trip to China the following year.

But tonight she was all mine, thank God. I got cranky when I didn't see her.

Miranda was stepping out of her car as I parked up. She waited for me. I also hadn't spoken to her properly since the party, beyond passing hellos and goodbyes.

She had her gossip face on. I smelled trouble.

"Did you know Dominic was at ours the other night? Forgot his watch on the night of the party."

"I don't know what he does most of the time," I said, disinterested. This wasn't the type of response one expected from a happy wife, but I didn't care anymore.

"He stayed for a drink. We had a very interesting talk about you."

My stomach did a lurch. Oh no, what had he told her? Did she know about me and Ava?

"You talked about me?"

"Ah-huh." She slapped a hand on my shoulder, chuckling. "Don't worry, it wasn't anything bad. We were just saying how brave you are, how progressive. You know, still remaining friends with Miss Petal."

I frowned. "Why wouldn't I still be friends with her?"

"Because she...you know, bats for the other team. It's good that you don't have a problem with that sort of thing."

"Miranda, it's the twenty-first century. There's nothing progressive or noble about having a gay friend." It hurt having this conversation with her of all people. Would she also consider herself progressive and noble for having me as a friend, if my affair ever got out?

"I'm just saying."

I changed the subject. But she jumped right back onto it a minute later while we were in the playground.

"She's a nice lady and all, but I don't know if a school is the right place for her, you know."

"What is that supposed to mean?" I felt sick now, close to throwing up. My good mood was sinking into the abyss. This was the elephant in the room Ava and I had been unable to discuss: Miranda, and others like her.

She didn't have enough time to respond, because the bell dinged, and moments later the doors swung open and the kids spilled out, running to their parents and guardians.

Chester came crashing into me with a hug, making me laugh. That always brightened up my day, even if only temporarily.

"Good day?" I asked, ruffling his hair, which was already as scruffy as ever.

He nodded and started telling me all about what he got up to. When Ava spotted me, she gave me a faint smile of greeting. A non-verbal cue that meant much more than anyone else would ever understand. Encompassed in that gesture was a declaration of her love for me. And my returned smile, my declaration of love for her.

"Miss Petal, I need to talk to you," came the sudden, angry shout of a mother, who was all but dragging her small daughter across the playground by the arm.

Everyone had stopped to look now. And despite being shouted at, Ava smiled politely. I swallowed, sensing that things were about to turn ugly.

"Did you put a band-aid on my daughter's knee?" the woman demanded. There was a bright-colored band-aid on said knee.

Ava frowned. "Yes. She fell over in class."

"And *you* had to be the one to put it on?"

She frowned deeper. "Yes, I'm her teacher. I didn't want her cut getting infected. Don't worry, I'm First Aid trained." She was trying to stay positive, trying to lighten the mood.

"You can't just go around touching our daughters like that. In future I'd like one of the other teachers to handle that sort of thing."

The blood seemed to drain from Ava's face; and I was sure from my own, too. Now almost the whole playground was watching and listening to her being condemned for doing her job. And I got the feeling everyone knew what this was about. That rumor hadn't taken very long to spread.

She couldn't have held onto that smile if she'd tried. And no one would have expected her to.

"You have a problem with me putting a band-aid on your daughter?"

"I'm not the only one." The woman held her daughter close, as though protecting her from the big, bad Ava. "It's not appropriate. I have no problem with you teaching our children, of course, because I'm not a bigot. But I draw the line at any type of physical contact."

"What exactly is it that you have a problem with, Mrs. Richter?" Her voice was cold, her stare even colder.

"Well... You know what. Parents talk. And we believe you should have disclosed details of your...*orientation* before you started teaching here. As I've said before, I'm not against you teaching our children–"

"On the contrary, Mrs. Richter, you seem to have a very big problem with it. And my "orientation", as you put it, is no one's business but my own. It has nothing at all to do with my ability to teach."

One of the father's stepped forward, a man who had been one of Ava's biggest fans, always striking up conversations with her in the mornings. He'd stopped doing that since the party. Still, I held out hope that he would at least see that what this woman was saying was madness, and come to Ava's defense.

"I do understand her concerns. I don't think it's right that you didn't disclose it. Some of us have daughters. We're concerned about their well-being."

You fucking asshole! I wanted to scream at him. *The only reason why you're so pissed off that she didn't disclose it is because you spent months trying to get into her pants.*

I couldn't believe what was happening.

"Mom, why is Sara's mom angry at Miss Petal?" Chester's big, doleful eyes peered up at me, almost tearful.

"Because she's being ignorant," I said quietly. "You remember what that word means, don't you? Miss Petal taught you."

He nodded.

"And you seem to think that your daughters are, what, in danger in my classroom? Because I'm gay?"

A circle of angry, "concerned" parents seemed to have formed around her now. They were like vultures. Like playground bullies. And although most stayed back, watched from the sidelines and said nothing, the small group was loud enough.

"I just don't want you putting your hands on my daughter, all right?" Mrs. Richter shouted.

"Nor do I. I don't want you getting ideas, or...or... Well, who knows what you people think like. And there I was thinking it was only male ones we had to watch out for." This disparaging remark came from another mother with a daughter, a crow-faced woman who, in the years that I'd known her, had always been complaining about something. But this was by far the worst I'd ever seen her. It was also this line, a line so sick, that made me finally step forward, weakly.

"All right, I think that's enough." My voice was shaky and uncertain. The pain in Ava's eyes was so obvious, so loud. I felt sick.

"It's all right for you, you have a son."

"Yeah. And how can you still defend her after what we know about her? You had better keep your distance lest you want people thinking you're like that too. Guilty by association."

My mouth and throat were as dry as the desert, and when I tried to speak, I found I couldn't. But it was the look that Ava gave me then, the look of complete and utter devastation, of lost hope, of despair, that cut like a knife. When she looked at me she saw betrayal. I turned away, kept silent.

"I must say," she said after a moment, addressing the outraged parents, "it's refreshing to know how you all think. Thank you." She disappeared back into the building. And I...I didn't go after her. Once again.

"What a bloodbath!" Miranda said as we made our way to our cars. "The claws really came out. I don't envy her. I mean, do people actually believe she'll harm their children?"

I couldn't speak. It wasn't too long ago that she'd expressed similar concerns to the others.

I didn't even say goodbye to her, just loaded Chester into the car.

"Mom, Miss Petal looked sad," he said, with a sadness of his own.

"I know, honey. I know."

I knew we were through even before I arrived at her house that evening. I was fully expecting her not to open the door when I knocked. Why would she want to see me? What I'd done, or failed to do, was despicable. Unforgivable.

But she did open it, and she did let me in. I looked at her face, saw the dried tear streaks. It killed me to see her like this. And when I reached out to stroke her face, she shoved my hand away.

"I know you're mad at me, Ava," I said, swallowing back tears of my own. "But please let me explain."

She gave a humorless laugh. "This feels a lot like déjà vu. We've been here before. Not so long ago."

"I'm sorry." The words sounded so pathetic and meaningless. I needed more, better ones, but what did you say to the woman you'd betrayed?

"Yeah, so am I." She was at her window spot. "They actually believe that just because I'm gay I'm some sort of pervert. That their kids need protecting from me. This isn't the first time something like this has happened. A little girl last week told me her mother said I wasn't allowed to touch her because it was "unhealthy". All I was doing was giving her a high five for getting a math question right..." She burst into tears.

My heart ached for her. And once again I tried to comfort her, but she shrugged me off.

"You don't get to do that anymore," she said. "You let them say those things to me and didn't once defend me. You're supposed to be my girlfriend, yet you stayed and watched me suffer. And remember, when they talk like that, they're talking about you, too."

"But I'm not gay." Oh God, wrong response. Wrong goddamn response. It was as though I'd erased everything we'd shared together. Erased our love in one simple sentence.

Through her tears, she looked at me in disgust. "Only when it suits you. Wow, that has got to be the fastest backtrack I've ever seen."

"What did you expect me to say?" I demanded. Her glare was ice cold and made me shiver. She'd once looked at me with nothing but love. Now it was hatred that filled her eyes. "Telling them I'm sleeping with you was hardly going to help either of us."

"You should have said something!" she screamed. "Anything would have been better than just standing there, as though you agreed with what they were saying."

I cast my eyes to the floor. Beneath my feet was the rug that we'd made love on. Where we'd also exchanged our first I Love Yous. It all seemed so long ago. In a sense, it was. We were past that now. There was no going back, or even moving forward. Not for us.

"I can't be what you need me to be, Ava," I said in a quiet, trembling voice.

"I just needed you to be there for me." She sounded defeated, all the fight gone from her voice. "I'd like you to leave, please." She didn't look at me when she said that.

I didn't move immediately. My legs felt numb. I wanted to tell her that I loved her and probably always would, but my mouth felt numb, too.

She tutted, then stormed from the room. "You can see yourself out then."

This end was inevitable, of course. Because of my cowardice. The truth was, I'd witnessed the ill treatment of an out lesbian, a woman I loved with all of my being, and knew I wasn't cut out for that life. Ostracized and shunned by friends and acquaintances. My marriage was a joke, a miserable pantomime, but it afforded me a privilege I had grown accustomed to. I'd spent so long trying to build the perfect life, worked so damn hard to maintain it, which meant putting up with Dominic. I'd destroyed relationships with my family in pursuit of it. My love for Ava wasn't enough to get me to walk away from all of that. It wasn't strong enough to make me brave.

I cried in my car, which was still parked across the street from her house. I could see her door. I wished I could have been the woman she wanted me to be. I prayed for a miracle. And then I drove home after an hour of bawling my eyes out all over the steering wheel. Home, to my life of privilege, and to a husband whom I hated.

NINETEEN

I didn't see Miss Petal at school for the remainder of the week. When I asked Chester where she was, he said she'd called in sick. They'd had a substitute.

It was easier for me that I didn't see her so soon after the break up. Perhaps easier for her, too. My heart ached too much, and seeing her would have only sought to remind me of what I'd lost. What I'd, in effect, given up.

Who could blame her for calling in sick, after the knives had come out? How quickly everyone had turned on her, as though they'd forgotten all the wonderful things she'd done for their children. Kids who had trouble with spelling were now able to spell. Likewise with math. I'd heard it time and again, what a miracle worker she was, the best teacher their children ever had. And they'd still turned on her, so unnecessarily, too.

I should have defended her.

It still haunted me that I didn't. That I wasn't dependable. It still stung that she thought of me as not her lover, but the woman who betrayed her. I vowed that in time I would summon the right words to say to her. I needed her to know that I did love her, I just wasn't strong enough to be with her. She could hate me for being weak, but not because she thought our time together meant nothing to me.

But when the new week began, and she failed to show up, it became apparent that she wasn't going to return. The principal confirmed at the end of the week that she had in fact resigned.

And so began the new cycle of substitute teachers, kids falling behind academically, and generally everything we all hated as parents, that had made us consider removing our children from the school.

We'd broken her. A woman who had been a breath of fresh air, to all of us, not just our children. We'd pushed her out. When I spoke to the principal he mentioned that she had decided to tutor privately until she got a new teaching post in a school. He seemed just as distraught to see her go as I was.

I had a lot to think about. Going back on the substitute merry-go-round wasn't an option. I didn't want that headache again, worrying about my son's academic future.

But something else troubled me when I learned of her resignation. Not just the thought of the instability in Chester's class, something even more personal. It had been a mere week and a half since I'd last seen her, and I was already crumbling. I missed her. My body missed her. I'd never banked on her leaving, and just assumed she would stick it out, and that we would see each other daily. Even though it would have been painful, not seeing her was far worse. *That* I wasn't prepared for.

It was Saturday evening when I drove down to her place. I had no right to be there, and she had every right to tell me to go to hell. But at least we would exchange words. I just needed to see her, even if it was a brief and heated exchange. She could call me all the names under the sun as long as she spoke to me.

I saw the living room light on through the window, heard

the faint sound of the television. She was in. I knocked. The television went silent, but I heard no more movement. I knocked and rang, more frantically this time.

"Ava, it's me, Danielle."

The television sound came back on, but this time the volume increased. She was blocking me out.

"Ava, please open the door. I just want to talk."

She never did.

My fists hurt from all the banging. A neighbor came out to tell me it was late, that I should be on my way. Making a scene wasn't my style, so I apologized and left, shooting one final, longing look at Ava's house. It felt a lot like the life I'd perfected for myself was slowly crumbling around me.

"What's up, buddy?" I asked Chester a couple of weeks later. We were at the dinner table, and he'd been wearing that glum expression since he got back home from school.

"May I be excused?"

"Not until you tell me what's wrong."

He let out a heavy sigh. "Do I have to go back to school?"

I laughed. "Of course you do, honey. You need an education."

"But school's no fun without Miss Petal."

I swallowed. Every time he mentioned her name, which was daily, I felt a pang in my chest.

Through the corner of my eye I saw Dominic smirking. It made me wish I'd given him a secret helping of dog food in his chilli con carne!

"Oh honey, you'll get another good teacher soon." It wasn't a promise I could make, and I wasn't at all convinced.

Chester also wasn't buying it. "No we won't. Miss Petal was the best."

"Your mom clearly doesn't think so. What happened, Dani,

you finally realized she didn't have the right parts to satisfy you?"

"You're disgusting," I said. Normally I kept comments like that to myself, but lately I'd been loath to do so. What was the point now? We couldn't raise Chester in a loving marriage – that was impossible to fake twenty-four hours a day – so the charade was redundant.

"Can we go see her?" Chester asked, big eyes filled with hope.

"She's busy, honey. She has a new job that takes up all of her time. I'm sure she misses you as much as you miss her, though."

Dominic snorted a laugh. "Who are we talking about here, Danielle? Him or you?"

Chester was still too young to understand what was being hinted at, and for that I was thankful. But the denigrating of his mother by his father was difficult to ignore at any age.

"It's not funny, Dad," he said, sulking.

"You can be excused now, honey. Go watch some TV." I waited until he had left the room before I exploded. "You... You shit!" It was the first thing that came to my head, and seemed to fit him well. "You disgusting pig! You are the worst human being I have ever had the displeasure of meeting. You think this is all a game, that it's funny what you started?"

"It's pretty funny, yes." He was laughing at me. My relationship was over, thanks to his intervention, and all he could do was laugh.

"You couldn't just let me be happy, could you? You couldn't let Chester be happy. He finally gets a teacher he likes, who's actually good for him, and you had to destroy that, you selfish piece of...of..."

"The kid will be fine. But you won't. Did you honestly think you could start fucking a woman, right under my nose, and I would let you get away with that?" Now he wasn't laughing, he had risen to his feet, and his face was the picture of pure disgust. "My son's teacher! I warned you not to try to make a fool of me, Danielle. I warned you. So your whore had to suffer."

"It was you, wasn't it? Who went to the principal and complained about our friendship?" It finally dawned on me. The thought had crossed my mind, but I didn't think he would have been so petty.

"And I made sure everyone at school learned about Lovely Miss Petal, the dyke who has a thing for much younger women." He grinned heinously. "I embellished a little there, but it did the job. Made them fear that their innocent daughters were in danger."

"Oh my God!" My body felt weak. My mouth hung open in shock. "You made them think she was a child molester... How could you be so sick?"

"I did what I had to do. If you think you get to run off with some gash you've only known a few months, you're wrong."

I wandered out of the room absentmindedly, so flabbergasted I couldn't speak, and still couldn't close my mouth. It was as though I was in a trance as I walked up the stairs and into my bedroom. Every action I did after that felt like I was being guided by some invisible force. Pulling open the closet door, filling my suitcase with clothes and essentials, then going into Chester's room and doing the same with his things.

I lugged Chester's suitcase out to the car first, and Dominic saw me.

"What the hell do you think you're doing?" he demanded when I came back in to collect my case.

"Something I should have done a long time ago. I'm leaving you." I was so calm, anyone who saw me then would have thought me insane. But I had never been more sane.

"Like hell you are," he said, and grabbed my wrist.

"If you don't get your hands off me, Dominic, I swear to God I'll scream this house down, and everyone in the neighborhood will know what sort of man you are. And any relationship you have with your son will be from behind a glass screen." He'd never been physically abusive to me, and this was not a good time to start. I would ruin his life if he ever tried to stop me from leaving.

"You're not taking my son anywhere." He let go.

"*My* son! He's my son, and he's coming with me. Now get the hell out of my way."

I got my case, loaded it into the trunk. In the living room, the furniture and electronics were being smashed and broken by my furious husband, who'd realized he'd lost. He'd banked on me not wanting to disturb my perfect life. And he'd gone too far. I couldn't live under the same roof as a man who could do something so disgraceful.

"Chester, come on, honey, get your coat on."

"Where are we going?"

"We're staying in a hotel while Mommy finds something more permanent."

"Is Dad coming?"

"No. You can see him in a few days."

I packed my son and myself into the car and sped off without glancing back at the house.

TWENTY

"It's nice. I like it. Has a homely feel to it," Beth said, giving her verdict on my new house. I'd just finished showing her around.

"That was the feel I was going for. Also, I needed something quick. I couldn't stay another night cooped up in that hotel room."

"You could have stayed with us, I told you that."

I made us coffees, then we sat down at the brand new dining table in the kitchen.

"I didn't want to put you guys out, or get you in the middle of the breakup."

She shook her head over and over. "I still can't believe you're separated. Nothing makes sense anymore."

"Well believe it. We'd been sleeping in separate beds for almost two years. Hadn't been intimate in just as long."

"So what happens now? The dreaded D-word?"

I smiled. Nothing about it was dreaded, not anymore. "Yup. I met with a lawyer yesterday. I want a clean break. A fresh start."

"No alimony?"

I shook my head. "He can provide for his son, but I want nothing from him."

"Wow." She sipped her coffee. "I hate that you didn't come to me with this when the affairs started."

"What would you have done?"

"I would have told you to cut his balls off!"

We laughed. It felt great to be able to come clean about the hell I'd been through with Dominic. I should have known Beth would be supportive.

"And how is Chester taking it?"

"Well, actually. They've seen each other a couple of times. He understands that we're not getting back together. He's adjusting to the new house, the new situation. Sadly, I wish I could say the same about school."

"Ugh, tell me about it. Miss Petal's only been gone a few weeks and I'm already seeing a marked deterioration in Jack's work. Why the hell did she have to leave?"

"You know why. Because a few bigots couldn't stand the fact that she's gay, and pushed her out," I said bitterly.

"Yeah but that was just a handful of idiots. Most people didn't give a damn. Well, apart from some of the disgruntled husbands who thought they had a shot with her."

"Most people didn't come to her defense." How hypocritical of me to condemn others for not doing what I'd also failed to do.

"It's a nightmare. If I'd been there I would have had her back. She's the best teacher that class is ever likely to get. Do you know what she's doing now?"

"I heard she's tutoring," I said casually.

"Hmm, so she's still in the field. Maybe I should give her a call, see if she'd be willing to give Jack some lessons."

After Beth had left, I jumped on my laptop. She'd given me an idea. I had tried to contact Ava several times since our split, even turned up at her house twice, but she either wasn't in or didn't want to speak to me.

I had her tutoring email address, which I'd obtained after some stealthy internet searching. I sent the message from my new email address, one that used my maiden name, a name she wasn't familiar with. I arranged a tutoring session with her. It was a genius idea. She didn't know about the new house, so would be none the wiser.

Three days later, half five, Chester was waiting in the dining room.

"Why do I need a tutor?" he asked.

"Because I don't want you to fall behind in school."

He wasn't happy about it. I smiled to myself imagining the look on his face when he saw who his new tutor was.

When the bell rang, my heart did a big leap. A queasy feeling settled in my stomach.

I pulled the door open slowly. Her face seemed to display just about every emotion imaginable in those few seconds when she realized I had tricked her. And then it settled on anger.

"What is this?"

"Hi," I said shyly.

"What is this, Danielle?" she asked again, this time with more force.

"Just hear me out. I'm sorry I tricked you into coming here. Well, it's not exactly a trick, I do want you to tutor, but–" I bumbled. I had this whole speech planned, and somewhere in it I was supposed to confess that I'd tried to live without her and couldn't. And also that I'd started divorce proceedings.

But she wasn't about to let me get that far into my declaration.

She held up a hand to silence me. "I don't care. And you shouldn't have done this."

"But don't you want to know why I'm here now? I left my

husband."

There was a flicker of something – surprise maybe – but it was faint and brief. She sighed. "Good for you. I have to go now."

"Miss Petal!" Chester turned up just in time, running out of the house and diving into her arms.

"Hey, Chester." She smiled sadly at him, but at me she glowered.

"Are you my tutor?"

"No, sweetie. I can't be your tutor. I'm sorry." She stroked his hair, then looked up at me. "That's not fair, Danielle. Not fair at all."

"He misses you. What did you expect? And I miss you too."

She separated herself from Chester, even though I could see how painful it was for her to do so. "I can't do this, I'm sorry."

She turned and started off quickly down the drive.

"Ava, please, don't go," I called, but she didn't stop. She climbed into her car and took off.

I cried myself to sleep that night. It was foolish of me to think that it would be that easy. I cried, clutching my pillow, convinced that what we had could no longer be salvaged.

I suppose the thing that continued to haunt me was that, despite Ava seeing that I had taken the huge step of leaving my husband, she'd remained mostly indifferent. Because the truth was, my move was about me, not about us. And although she had a lot to do with it, it was something I would have eventually done whether or not she'd entered my life.

So in that respect, nothing had really changed. It didn't change the past, namely my failure to come to her defense, to be there for her when she needed me the most. She'd seen who I really was: a coward who hated myself and what I was. If she couldn't depend on me, what was the point?

But I refused to believe that she had stopped loving me. I was stubborn like that. If she had ever felt as strongly for me as I did for her, the flame of our love would still be burning strong in her heart. And while it did, there was still a chance for me to win her back. Still hope for us. That belief was one of the only things that got me up each morning.

Seeing as my last attempt to get her to talk to me again hadn't worked, I had to come up with something bigger. Better. Something she couldn't just walk away from.

And then I had it.

Miranda was the first person on my list. If I could get through to her, she could help me with the others.

"They were pretty nasty to her. I don't think anything we say could change her mind. And I wouldn't blame her," Miranda said of my new plan, as we stood in the playground waiting for the kids to come out.

"I mean, we're all suffering for it now," she continued. "Our kids are. And the finger pointing has started. The ones that attacked her are being blamed for ruining their kids' futures. Lots of remorse. She would feel pretty self-satisfied right now knowing how screwed we are without her."

"She wouldn't be. She's not like that," I said sadly. "She actually cared about the kids; if they're suffering, it won't please her."

"It's a good plan, I guess." She shrugged. "We can probably get most of the parents to go along with it. And you know the kids will be up for it."

I looked at her seriously. "We don't need most, we need *all*. I know some of them are homophobic apes, but for this to work they all have to be on board."

"That might be tricky."

"It won't be if they care about their children."

She looked at me. "This really means a lot to you, doesn't

it?"

I fought back my tears and nodded. "I just hope it works."

It was the last day of the semester, and a couple of hours before the end of school. I pulled up outside Ava's house. No hesitating, no hiding out in my car in order to build my courage. The past few weeks had seen me at my most courageous. My nerves weren't going to stand in the way of this.

I knocked the door, the DVD clasped tightly in my hand. I'd watched it several times, watched thirty-eight little faces declare how much they loved and missed their "favorite teacher in the whole world". How much she'd taught them and how much they wanted her to come back next semester.

I'd heard from many of the parents, Mrs. Richter among them, how ignorant and foolish they'd been, or how well their children worked with her. Even heard from the principal and staff, saying how much they loved her faculty jokes, her infectious laugh, and her positive energy.

Every heart she'd ever touched in that school was represented on that DVD. Only mine was missing.

I knocked and knocked. I heard movement upstairs but she didn't come to open the door.

I crouched down at the mailbox, pushed the flap open. "If you're not going to listen to me, listen to them." I dropped the DVD in. "They can say it better than I can. If you really don't care, then so be it. But if you do, you'll know what to do."

I walked back to my car, praying that her curiosity would get the better of her. I had so much riding on the recording. We all did. Seeing Chester had upset her before, but not enough for her to stay and tutor him. But thirty-eight adoring students... I hoped that overwhelming amount of love would be too much for her to ignore.

"Did you give it to her?" Beth asked that afternoon in the playground. She and Miranda waited with bated breath for my answer.

"Yes, but she didn't want to speak to me. I dropped it through her mailbox." I let out a dejected sigh. "I guess it wasn't enough. I really thought it would be."

"She might surprise us next semester. Who knows?" Miranda shrugged.

"She planned to go back to Bolivia in the summer. There's a very real chance she won't come back." I felt sick again. If she moved there I would lose her forever. She would forget me. The thought was almost too much to bear. I became a little lightheaded.

The bell rang. There was that almost ominous silence that passed as we all waited for our kids to be released. Several of the older classes were the first to come out. And then came Chester's class. I spotted him and he started toward me. And then he looked right past me. His eyes grew wide as saucers, and the largest smile spread across his face.

"Miss Petal!"

He wasn't the only one now running straight past their parents to their former teacher, who was standing at the gate. She was like the Pied Piper of Hamelin, leading thirty-eight adoring kids to her.

"Looks like it worked," Beth said, glee in her voice.

Within seconds they had swarmed her, hugs coming from all directions, from every child. She chuckled and hugged them back.

I just stood there, immobilized, a million different thoughts running through my head.

She was here! I'd gotten through to her. She was more beautiful than ever, surrounded by the love of her old class.

Moments later a few of the parents who had condemned

her several weeks prior, and had forced her to resign, approached her. There were sorries and handshakes, and lots of shame on their faces. They knew how badly they'd messed up. Apologizing was the least they could do.

And then she looked at me. We looked at each other. I walked towards her, and she stepped out of the crowd of joyous kids.

I didn't have to think about my next move. She opened her mouth to speak, and I moved in, smashed my lips to hers. It was a kiss without tongue, kept PG because of the setting. I heard gasps and laughter around us. In my peripheral vision I saw a few disapproving faces, but none of that mattered now.

"I love you," I declared, loud enough so everyone could hear. "And I promise that from now on I'll always support you. As your partner. As your girlfriend."

She smiled, the smile that had made me fall in love with her in the first place. I vowed that I would work day and night to make sure it never faded again.

Novels by Heidi Lowe

Beautiful Sin Saga
My Beautiful Sin
Sinning Again
Sinning Forever

Crave
The Queen of Miami
Strummed
Her Lesson in Love
A Scarlet Kiss
Before You Were Mine

For exclusive content, discounts, and news of upcoming titles, visit **www.hlowebooks.com**.

Made in the USA
Las Vegas, NV
05 December 2020